Molly Brown's Orchard Home

Nell Speed

MOLLY BROWN'S
ORCHARD
HOME

NELL SPEED

MOLLY BROWN'S ORCHARD HOME

By NELL SPEED

AUTHOR OF

"The Tucker Twins Series," "The Carter Girls Series," etc.

1915

Jo proved to be a singularly tactful hostess.

CONTENTS

Other books by A.L. Burt Company

CHAPTER I.

LETTERS.

From Miss Molly Brown of Kentucky to Miss Nance Oldham of Vermont.

Chatsworth, Kentucky.

My dearest Nance:

Our passage to Antwerp is really engaged and in two weeks Mother and I will be on the water. I can hardly believe it is I, Molly Brown, about to have this "great adventure." That is what Mother and I call this undertaking: "Our great adventure." Mother says it sounds Henry Jamesy and I take her word for it (so far I have not read that novelist), but he must be very interesting, as Mother and Professor Green used to discuss him for hours at a time.

Our going is not quite so happy as we meant it to be. Kent can't come with us as we had planned, but will have to stay in Louisville for some months, and may not be able to leave at all this winter. There is some complication of our affairs, that makes it best for him to be on hand until the matter is settled. I remember how interested you were in the fact that oil was found on my mother's land and that she expected to realize an independent income from the sale of the land, also pay off the mortgage on Chatsworth, our beloved home. Don't be too uneasy, the oil is there all right enough and we shall finally get the money, but the arrangement was: so much down and the rest when the wells should begin operation.

The first payment Mother used immediately to pay the mortgage, but the second payment has not been made yet, as Mother's sister, Aunt Clay, living on the adjoining place, has got out an injunction against the Oil Trust as a public nuisance, and all work in the oil land has had to be stopped for the time being. The lawyer for the Trust told my brother, Paul, that Aunt Clay has not a leg to stand on, but of course the law has to take its leisurely course, and in the meantime the money for Mother is not forthcoming until the wells are in operation. Aunt Clay is in her element, making everyone as uncomfortable as possible and engaged in a foolish lawsuit. She is always going to law about something and always losing. We are devoutly thankful that her suit is with the Trust and not our Mother, as we know that Mother is so constituted she could not stand up against a member of her family in a lawsuit. I truly believe she would let Aunt Clay take the oil lands and all the rest of Chatsworth, rather than have a row over it.

This property, where the oil was found, was given to Mother by Aunt Clay when she settled up Grandfather Carmichael's estate. Of course she considered the property of no value or she would never have let it out of her clutches, and as executrix and administratrix of the estate she had absolute power. Now that she sees it is worth more than all the rest put together, she is in such a rage with Mother that it is really absurd. She does not want us to go to Paris and is furious at the idea of Kent's "stopping work," as she calls it. She has got out this injunction just to keep us from going, I believe, as she is intelligent enough to know there is no use in trying to get ahead of a mighty Trust, and they will have to win in the end; but she had an idea that we would not go unless we had plenty of money to have a good time on. She little knows our Mother, in spite of being her sister.

Mother says she believes it will be more fun and easier to economize in Paris than in Kentucky; and she is as gay as a lark over the prospect. Kent may be able to come later and take that much talked of and longed for course in Architecture at the Beaux Arts. In the meantime, he is very busy and, as he says, "making good with his boss." Mother refuses to discuss Aunt Clay's behavior and actually goes to see her as though nothing had happened; but I know she has had many a sleepless night, brooding over her sister's unsisterly act.

I am longing to see you, dearest Nance, and wish you could manage to meet me in New York before we sail, but if you can't, be sure to have a letter on the steamer for me. We are going on a slow boat to Antwerp. We think the long sea trip will be good for Mother, who is tired out with all this worry and the work of getting Chatsworth in condition to leave; and besides, the slow boats are much cheaper. *Laurens* is the name of our boat, sailing from Hoboken. I will write you from Paris, where Julia Kean is already installed and hard at work on her beloved art.

I am afraid you will think I am horrid about Aunt Clay. Mother says she is the only person she ever knew me to feel bitter about. So she is, but then she is the only person who was ever mean to my beloved Mother. Maybe when my hair turns gray I can be as much of a lady as Mother is, but so far I am too red-headed to be a perfect lady.

I am going to miss you, Nance, more than I can tell you. We have been roommates for five years at college, and never once did we have a shadow of a disagreement. Of course we occasionally got in a kind of penumbra. Once I remember when I was touchy because you called Professor Edwin Green an oldish person, but my pettishness only lasted "like a cloud's flying shadow," and that ought not to count.

I think you are splendid to make such a happy home for your father and I know you are a wonderful housekeeper. Please give him my kindest regards. Kent drove Mother and me into Louisville to hear your mother speak at the Equal Suffrage Convention. She was simply overpowering in her arguments, and converted Kent in five minutes. I wish Aunt Clay, who is such an ardent Anti, had heard her. We were so sorry Mrs. Oldham could not come out to Chatsworth to visit us, but she did not have the time. I must stop. I have written two stamps' worth already.

Ever your devoted friend and roommate in heart,

MOLLY BROWN.

To Miss Molly Brown, Chatsworth, Kentucky,

From Miss Julia Kean, Paris, France.

71 Boulevard St. Michel, Paris.

Molly dear:

The news that you and your mother are to sail in a few weeks threw me into the seventh heaven of happiness,—I am already on the seventh floor of a *pension* with not much more of an elevator than the tower of Babel had. Mamma and Papa brought me here and installed me and then shot off to Turkey, Papa like a comet and Mamma like the tail of one, to finish up the bridge that has kept them so busy for the last year.

This *pension* is kept by an American lady and is full of Americans. It is rather fun to be here for a while, but I am longing for the time to come when you will be with me and we can go apartment hunting, that is, if your mother still thinks it will be wiser for us to keep house and not try to board. Of course you will come here first and we can take our time about getting settled for the winter. Mrs. Pace, the landlady, (but you had better not call her that to her face, as she is very much the *grande dame*, with so much blue blood she finds it difficult to keep it to herself,) wants you to stay all winter with her and has many arguments against housekeeping, but I'll let her get them off herself to your mother.

She is looking forward with great interest to meeting dear Mrs. Brown, as it seems she knows intimately a cousin and old friend of hers, a certain Sally Bolling of Kentucky, who is now the Marquise d'Ochtè, a swell of the Faubourg St. Germain, with a chateau in Normandy, family ghost, devoted peasantry and what not. I fancy your mother has told you of her. It will be great fun to meet some of the nobility, I think.

I am enrolled at the Julien Academy for the winter and am going to put in some months of hard drawing before I jump into color. I work only in the morning and spend the afternoons looking at pictures. I am such a sober person pacing the long galleries of the Louvre studying the wonderful paintings that no one would dream I am the harum-scarum I really am. Papa gave me a very serious talking to about how to conduct myself in Paris and I find, as usual, his advice is excellent. His theory is that any grown woman can go anywhere she wants to alone in Paris, provided she has some business to attend to and attends to it.

Of course Mrs. Pace is merely a nominal chaperone for me until your mother comes. She really seldom sees me, and when she does she is so full of her own affairs that she hardly remembers I have any; and then when she recalls that she is supposed to be my chaperone, she feels called upon to tell me to do my hair differently, or she does not

4

like my best hat, or something else equally out of her province. But I am not going to tell you any more about her, as you can judge for yourself when you see her.

I am sorry your brother, Kent, cannot carry out his plan of studying at the Beaux Arts, but maybe something will turn up and he can come after all. I might have known Aunt Clay would obstruct, all she had in her power, but thank goodness, her power is limited and your mother will finally get the full amount of money for her oil lands that Papa thought she should have. As for being in Paris without much money, it really is a grand place to be poor in; and one can have more fun here on a franc than in New York on a dollar.

Hug your darling mother for me, and tell Kent that I refuse to answer his letters unless he gets some thin paper to write on. I am tired of paying double extra postage on his bulky epistles.

Let me know in plenty of time when to expect you and your mother, so I can engage the room of Mrs. Pace and meet you at the station. I wish I could go to Antwerp to be there when you arrive or even meet you halfway in Brussels, but I must put the temptation from me and await you quietly in Paris. Good-by, my darling old Molly Brown,

Your own devoted, ever loving

JUDY.

Steamer letter from Professor Edwin Green of Wellington College to Miss Molly Brown of Kentucky, sailing on *S. S. Laurens.*

Wellington College.

My dear Miss Molly:

Surely the "best laid schemes of mice and men gang aft aglee." I feel more like a mouse caught in a trap than a man, just now. I have been thinking of nothing else all summer but the delightful time I should have with you and your mother in Paris. It is my sabbatical year at

Wellington, which means a fine long holiday, one much needed and looked forward to by all hard-worked professors. But just as I began to prepare for this delightful trip, I found that my substitute had in the most unaccountable manner, disappointed the President, Miss Walker, and Wellington was in a fair way to open without a professor of English. Of course I had to rush to the rescue and here I am in the old grind again.

I really do not mind teaching, enjoy it, in fact, but oh, my holiday and those walks and jaunts I have been dreaming of in Paris! Miss Walker is deeply grateful to me for helping her out of this difficulty, and is doing all in her power to find a suitable person to take my place; and of course, I, too, am reaching out in every direction for help.

One thing, I do not intend to be like poor Jacob: serve seven years more before I get my reward. I feel in a way that this is making up to the College for the long, enforced holiday two years ago, when I was so ill with typhoid fever.

My sister Grace had made her plans to spend the winter in New York as she did not expect to be needed by me as housekeeper, so I am "baching" again; and very lonesome it is after being so spoiled and looked after by Grace.

The place seems sad and gloomy to me and the College is full of raw and unattractive girls. I could hardly refrain from throwing a copy of Rosetti at a forward miss the other day in class, when she attempted to read "The Blessed Damozel" and I remembered a certain little Freshman, who, five years ago, held me enthralled by her rendering of that wonderful poem.

I was delighted to see your friend Miss Melissa Hathaway, who is a relief indeed, after all of these chattering school girls. What a wonderful personality she has! Her beauty is even richer and more glowing than formerly. She reminds me of October in the mountains, her own Kentucky mountains. Did you ever notice her eyes and the quality they possess, which is a very rare one: that of seeming to hold the reflection of trees and skies when she is indoors? It is as though she were still seeing her forests at home.

I hope to help her a great deal in her English as she is afraid this will have to be her last year at college. She feels that she is needed at home to carry on the work of her friend and teacher Miss Allfriend, whose long and arduous labors among the mountain folk have impaired her health. Melissa thinks she should take up the work and give her friend a rest. Noble girl! Dicky Blount thinks so, too, and even more so. Did you know that he found or manufactured some business in Catlettsburg, Kentucky, last summer and surprised Miss Hathaway in her mountain fastness?

Please give my kindest regards to your mother and express to her my deep regret that I am not to be her cicerone for some of the sights of Paris. I am hoping that before the winter is over I may be relieved and then, ho, for the fastest steamer afloat!

I am sending you some novels that may amuse you both on your voyage; also, a box of crystallized ginger that is the very best thing for seasickness that I know,—not that you are to be seasick, but just in case.

I am trying to be cheerful and not let Miss Walker see how I am kicking at fate, but I am as mad as a schoolboy who has to do chores on Saturday! Very sincerely your friend,

EDWIN GREEN.

CHAPTER II.

BON VOYAGE.

Mrs. Brown and her daughter Molly were at last safely off on what they called their "great adventure." They had waved their handkerchiefs until the dock at Hoboken was nothing more than a blur to them and they felt sure that the *Laurens* was little more than a speck to the friends that had turned up to see them off.

Molly's classmates at Wellington College, Katherine and Edith Williams, Edith with the nice, new husband whom Molly was overjoyed to meet, had appeared, bearing books and candy for the trip. Jimmy Lufton, of course, just to show that there was no hard feeling, as he whispered to Molly, was there, also, doing everything for their comfort; finding their luggage; engaging the steamer chairs; seeing to it that the stewardess understood about the baths before breakfast; and attending to many things of the importance of which Molly and her mother were ignorant.

Richard Blount, too, had turned up ten minutes before sailing, but he had managed to get in a word with Molly about Melissa Hathaway.

"She is a queen among women, Miss Molly, and I consider that Edwin Green is a lucky dog to have the privilege of teaching her. To think of seeing her day after day and hearing her read poetry with that wonderful voice! He tells me she is the most remarkable reader he has ever known. I am too fond of old Ed to hate him, otherwise I should find it easy. By the way I have left something in care of the steward for you and your mother as a cure for seasickness. You will find that there is nothing like it!"

"Oh, thank you so much! I feel sure that I shall not be sick, but I am just as obliged as though I were going to be. Mother may be. You see we have never been on the ocean in our lives, but we have always felt that we would like it beyond anything, and that liking it so much would keep us from being harmed by it," Molly had answered, a little chagrined at what Richard Blount had had to say about

8

Professor Green and Melissa, but determined not to show it to that young man or to let herself think there was anything in it.

Miss Grace Green and dear, good Mary Stewart had been on the steamer waiting when Molly and her mother came aboard. Their devotion to Molly was so apparent that they won Mrs. Brown's heart at once, and that charming lady with her cordial manner and gracious bearing as usual made Molly's friends hers.

Miss Green had had a little private talk with Molly, giving her messages from her younger brother, Dodo, and telling her what she knew of Professor Edwin's disappointment in having to go on with his duties for the time being at least. Molly had not had a chance to open and read the steamer letter he had written her, but was forced to postpone it until the vessel sailed and she could compose herself after the flurry of good-bys and the bustle of the departure.

There were many letters waiting in the cabin, but the harbor was so fascinating to these two women who had done so little traveling, that they could not tear themselves from the deck until they were out of sight of land.

"Mother, isn't it too lovely and aren't we going to be the happiest pair on earth? I am glad we are seeing the ocean for the first time together, because you know exactly how I feel and I know how you feel. The idea of our being seasick! Richard Blount sent some remedy to the steamer for us, just in case we were seasick. It was very kind of him but absolutely unnecessary, I am sure. I never felt better in my life and look, there is quite a little swell."

"Seasick indeed! I have no more feeling of sickness than I have on the Ohio River at home," said Mrs. Brown, taking deep breaths of the bracing salt air. "I suspect it is incumbent upon us to go read our letters now, but I must say I do not want to miss one moment on deck during our entire voyage. I feel as though twenty years had dropped off me." And indeed she looked it, too, with a pretty pink in her cheeks and her wavy hair blown about her face.

Molly rather wanted to read Professor Green's letter first, but she put it aside and opened those from Nance Oldham and several other college mates. Then she discovered a thoroughly characteristic note from Aunt Clay, dry and dictatorial but enclosing a check for ten dollars on Monroe & Co., the Paris bankers. "For you and your extravagant mother to spend on foolishness," wrote that stern lady.

"Oh, Mother! Isn't she hateful? How easy it would have been to send a pleasant message with the check! Now all the fun of having it is gone and I have a great mind to send it back!"

"No, my dear, don't do that. Your Aunt Clay does not mean to be as unkind as she seems. I know she intended this check as a kind of peace offering to me, and we must take it as she meant it and pay no attention to her words."

"Mother, you are an angel and I have to hug you right here in the cabin, even if that black-eyed man over there with the pile of telegrams in front of him is looking a hole through us."

She suited the action to the word and Mrs. Brown, emerging from the bear hug that Molly was prone to give, surprised a smile on the dark face of their fellow traveler. He was seated across from them at the same table behind a pile of telegrams a foot high, and was very busy opening the messages, making notes on them as he read. He was an interesting looking man with dark, fathomless eyes, swarthy complexion and iron gray hair, but he bore a youthful look that made one feel he had not the right of years to the gray hair. His expression was gloomy and not altogether pleasant, but when he smiled he displayed a row of dazzling white teeth and his eyes lost the sad look and held the smile long after his mouth had closed with a determined click.

"'Duty before pleasure,' as King Richard said when he killed the old king before a-smothering of the babies," said Molly as she finished Aunt Clay's letter and opened Edwin Green's. What a nice letter it was to be sure! She laughed aloud over his wanting to throw Rosetti at the girl and blushed with pleasure at the compliment to her reading of the blessed Damozel, for well she knew whom he had in mind. His praise of Melissa would have merely pleased her as praise of her friends always did, had she not already been somewhat disturbed by what Dicky Blount had said to her of Professor Edwin Green and the beautiful mountain girl.

"I am a silly girl and intend to put all such foolish notions out of my head," declared Molly to herself. "Surely Professor Green has as much right to make friends as I have, and I intend to know as many people and like as many as I can. I am not the least bit in love with Edwin Green,—but somehow I don't think he and Melissa are suited to one another."

As the young girl sat reading over her letter, a feeling of sadness and loneliness took possession of her and, looking up, she surprised a furtive tear in her mother's eye. Mrs. Brown was reading a letter from her married daughter Mildred, then living in Iowa where her husband Crittenden Rutledge was at work as a bridge engineer.

The cabin had begun to fill with people who were leaving decks and staterooms to hunt up their letters and belongings and generally prepare themselves for a ten-day trip on the Atlantic.

"Mother, they say this is a small steamer, but it seems huge to me! Did you ever see so many strange people? I don't believe we ever shall know any of them. They all of them look at home and I feel so far from home. Don't you?"

"Now, Molly, please don't get blue or I shall have to weep outright. Of course we shall come to know most of the passengers and no doubt will find many charming persons ready to know and like us. Suppose we hurry up with our letters and go on deck again."

Just then a young man bounded into the cabin, made a hasty survey of the crowd and came rapidly over to the dark gentleman seated opposite them.

"Oh, Uncle Tom, how can you stay down in this stuffy cabin? There is a sunset on the water that is just screaming out to be looked at. As for that work, you have ten days to attend to those tiresome telegrams and letters."

"Nonsense, Pierce, I have no idea of waiting ten days for this important business. You forget the wireless," answered the uncle,

11

looking fondly at the enthusiastic young fellow, who was so like him except for the gray hair that it was almost ludicrous.

"Oh, goodness gracious me, where is your holiday to be, with you tied to your Mother Country with a stringless apron? That is what that old wireless telegraphy reminds me of," laughed the young man, showing all his perfect teeth. "Well, I've got your chair and steamer rug all ready for you and all you have to do is come sit in it."

"Now, Pierce, don't wait on me. Part of having a holiday is to forget how old I am. When I get these telegrams off, I am going to show you how skittish I can be and forget all about business. I fancy you will have to hold me back in my race for a good time. This limerick is to be my motto:

"Said this long-legged daddy of Troy,
'Although I'm no longer a boy,
I bet I can show
You chaps how to go.'
Which he did to his own savage joy."

Mrs. Brown and Molly could not help overhearing this conversation and at the above limerick they laughed outright. The young man called Pierce looked at them with a friendly glance and the uncle smiled another of his rare smiles, which made the ladies from Kentucky feel that the ocean was not going to be such a terribly lonesome place after all. They gathered up their belongings and made their way on deck to view the sunset that was "screaming to be looked at."

"It really is worth seeing, isn't it, Mother? Somehow, though, I never do like to be made to look at a sunset. The persons who insist on your doing it always seem to have a kind of proprietary air. Now that young man wanted to bulldoze his uncle into coming when—when——" Molly stopped suddenly, realizing that the two men in great-coats, with the collars turned up to their ears, who had taken their places at the railing next to her mother, were no other than the two in question.

"You are perfectly right, madam," said the elder, raising his hat. "This nephew of mine is always doing it. Now I should much rather come on deck when the sun is down and see the after-glow. The crepuscule appeals to me more than the brilliancy of the sunset."

"I fancy my daughter had no complaint to make of the brilliancy of the color, but of being coerced into looking at it. She likes to be the discoverer herself and the one to make others come to look. Isn't it so, Molly?"

"Maybe it is," said Molly blushing. "I did not really mean much of anything and was just talking for talk's sake."

"Anyhow," spoke the nephew, "this sunset is mine and I think it is beautiful and all of you have simply got to look at it." Turning to Molly, "You can have to-morrow's and make us look all you want to, but this is my discovery."

The ice was broken and Molly and her mother made their first acquaintances on their travels. Mr. Kinsella introduced himself and his nephew Pierce and in the course of half an hour they were all good steamer friends. Everyone must make up his or her mind to be ready to make friends on a steamer or to have a very stupid, lonesome crossing. Mrs. Brown and Molly were both too sociable and friendly to be guilty of such standoffishness and were as pleased at making friends with the two Kinsellas as those gentlemen were to secure such pleasant companions as these ladies were proving themselves to be.

"We are all of us to be at the captain's table," said Pierce.

"And how do you know where we are to be?" asked Molly. "I don't know myself where we are to sit, and how can you know?"

"Oh, that is easy. While you and your mother and Uncle Tom were busy reading your letters and before I got my sunset ready, I was finding out things like Rikki-tikki. First I got the steward's list and located the Kinsellas at mess; then I looked over all the names and where the people hailed from and decided that Miss Molly Brown of Kentucky sounded kind of cheerful. And when I knew there was a Mrs. Brown along, too, I decided that Miss Molly Brown was young enough to have a mother along and the mother was young enough to be along, and you were more than likely a pretty nice couple to cultivate. The steward told me you were to be at the captain's table, too, as you were friends of Miss Mary Stewart. Her father owns much stock in these nice old tubs of steamers, and the daughter had made a special request that you should be very well looked after."

"Isn't that too like Mary? She did not say one word about it. That accounts for our having such a lovely stateroom to ourselves, too. We had engaged a stateroom that was supposed to hold three persons. The company had the privilege of putting someone else in with us, and as the steamer is quite full, of course we had expected to have a roommate. We hated the thought of it, too, but it was so much less expensive. And Mother and I hoped to spend most of our time on deck, anyhow. We could not understand the number not being the same as that on our tickets, but thought the officials knew best and if we did not belong there they would oust us in good time."

"Well, I am jolly glad you have the best stateroom on board. Uncle tried to get it but had to content himself with second best."

"Are you seasick, as a rule? I do hope not," asked the young man of Mrs. Brown, who had been conversing with Mr. Kinsella while the nephew and Molly were making friends.

"No, we don't make it a rule to be any kind of sick; but my daughter and I are on the ocean for the first time. In fact, we are really seeing the ocean for the first time and do not know how we are to behave. So far we feel as well as possible, but I fancy such a smooth sea is no test."

"Only fancy, Uncle Tom, what it must seem to see the ocean for the first time! I almost wish I had never seen it until now, just for the sensation."

"There was a superior New York girl at Wellington College who had a great time trying to tease me because I had never seen the ocean. She kept it up so long that I began to feel like a 'po' nigger at a frolic', so I retaliated by asking her if she had ever been to a hanging. I completely took the wind out of her sails, and then confessed that I hadn't either," said Molly with a laugh.

"Good for you, Miss Brown, give it to him. New York people are certainly very superior in their own estimation and need a good taking down every now and then. They are often more provincial than villagers, with no excuse for so being," and Mr. Kinsella gave his nephew an affectionate push.

The air was clear and crisp, with a rising wind that gave promise of a heavy sea. The passengers had begun to fill the decks, dragging steamer chairs into sheltered nooks and looking about for desirable places out of the wind, where they could see the sun set and the moon rise, get out of the way of the smokestacks, the fog horn and the whistle, and at the same time be in a good locality to see everything that was going on. Molly and her mother were much amused at the sight. They were both inclined to be rather careless of their ease and it had never entered their heads to hustle and bustle to make themselves comfortable on the trip.

"Jimmy Lufton has had our chairs placed on deck and lashed to the railing. He said he knew we would never look out for ourselves, and unless he saw to it, we would go abroad standing up or sitting on the floor! He tagged our chairs, too, as our names were on the backs only. He said there were always some 'chair hogs' who would push the chairs against the wall with the name out of sight and refuse to budge," said Molly.

"Where are your chairs?" asked Pierce. "Let's go find them and afterward we can get Uncle's and mine and have a snug foursome of a chat. Oh, Miss Brown, how lovely your mother is! I want to paint her; but I should have to put you in the picture, too, so that I could catch the wonderful expression on her face. It is when she is looking at *you* that she is most lovely."

"Well, don't you think I could be present to inspire the desired expression without being in the picture?" laughed Molly, delighted by the praise of her beloved mother. "But can you paint? I have been wondering what you are and what your uncle is, but I did not like to be too inquisitive."

"Well, one does not have to be with me long to hear the story of my life," said the boy. "You ask if I can paint: yes, I can paint; not as well as I want to by a long shot, but I mean to be a great painter. That sounds conceited, but it is not. I have talent and there is no use in being mealy-mouthed over it. To be a great painter means work, work, work; and I am prepared to do that with every breath I breathe. Painting isn't work to me; it is joy and life. Besides, I mean to make it up to Uncle for his disappointment in life, and the only way I can do it is by succeeding."

Molly was dying to know more about the uncle and what his disappointment was, but she was too well bred to show her desire and Pierce did not seem inclined to go on with his family disclosures. He stood looking at two ladies who had just come on deck, followed by a maid carrying rugs and cushions. The ladies were a very handsome mother and daughter, although the mother appeared too young to have such a very sophisticated, grown-up daughter. They were beautifully dressed in long fur coats and small toques. "Rather warm for October," thought Molly, but the rising cold wind soon made her know her mistake.

"There are our chairs," said Molly, starting toward the railing where the ever handy-man, Jimmy, had lashed the two steamer chairs.

At the same moment the elegant, fur-clad lady rapidly crossed the deck and placing her hand on the back of the nearest chair, said in a cold and haughty tone to the maid: "Here, Marie, place the rugs and cushions in these chairs. They will do quite nicely."

"Excuse me, but these chairs are ours, mine and my mother's," said Molly. "But we are not going to use them until after supper, I mean dinner, so you are welcome to them until then."

"Some mistake surely," rejoined the older woman, eying Molly scornfully through her lorgnette. "You will have to complain to the steward if you cannot find your chairs, young woman; these are mine, engaged and paid for." With that, she prepared to seat herself with the help of the maid, who was blushing furiously, mortified by the flagrant untruth of her mistress.

Molly was, by nature, easy-going and peace-loving and her inclination was to leave the haughty dame in possession of the chairs and beat a hasty retreat; but she remembered Jimmy Lufton's remark about "chair hogs" and a joking promise she had made him to stand up for her mother if not for herself, so she braced herself for battle. Despite her girlish face and figure, Molly Brown could command as much dignity as any member of the Four Hundred.

With a polite smile and gently modulated voice she said, very calmly and firmly: "Madam, as I said before, these are my chairs but you are quite welcome to them until after dinner. If you have any doubt about it, you will find our names on the backs; but to save you the trouble of moving to look behind you, if you will be so kind as to glance at these tags you can verify my statement."

"Oh, I did not dream I was to call forth such a tirade," yawned the nonplussed woman, reading the tags: "'Mrs. M. Brown, Kentucky; Miss M. Brown, Kentucky.' If you are not going to use the chairs until after dinner, my daughter and I will just stay in them until other arrangements can be made. These small steamers are wretchedly managed. I can't imagine where our chairs are. Elise," calling to her daughter, "it seems these are not our chairs, after all."

"Well, I did not think they could be, as these chairs seem real enough and ours are entirely imaginary," answered the daughter rudely. "Mother, this is Mr. Kinsella, whom I have known at the Art Students' League. My mother, Mrs. Huntington, Mr. Kinsella."

"I am so glad to meet you, Mrs. Huntington. Your daughter, Miss O'Brien, and I have been working in the same costume class at the League. I did not dream she was to be on this boat and when I saw her come on deck I thought I was seeing ghosts."

Pierce had come eagerly forward to meet the mother of the interesting girl he had known and liked at the art school; but Mrs. Huntington looked as though she, too, were seeing ghosts. She shrank back in her down pillows and her face became pinched and pale, and it was a moment before the hardened woman of the world could command her voice to return the greeting of the young man.

17

"Kinsella, did you say? Could you be Tom Kinsella's son? You are strangely like him."

"Thank you, madam, for that. There is no one I want to be like so much as my Uncle Tom. I am his nephew; my uncle has never married. Did you know my uncle? He is on board and I know would be glad to renew his acquaintance with you. But let me introduce Miss Brown to both of you."

The two girls shook hands, and as they looked in each other's eyes, Molly felt in her heart an instinctive liking for the older girl. There was something honest and straight about her face despite the rather sullen expression of her mouth. She was beautiful, besides, and beauty always appealed to Molly,—almost always, at least, for although Mrs. Huntington was beautiful, too, Molly felt no leaning toward her. Mother and daughter looked enough alike to make it not difficult to guess the relationship at the first glance; but the more one saw of them, the fainter grew the resemblance. The older woman was smaller, fairer and plumper; her hair was golden while the daughter's was light brown; her complexion pink and white, the daughter's rather sallow; her eyes baby blue, the other's gray green. But the daughter's features were more pronounced and her well-cut chin and mouth showed character and pride, while the mother's looked a little petulant.

"I am very glad to meet you, Miss Brown. I believe I have heard of you. Aren't you Julia Kean's 'Molly'?" And Elise O'Brien gave Molly's hand a little squeeze.

"Of course I am. To think of your knowing my Judy! You must have met her at the League. Perhaps you knew her, too, Mr. Kinsella."

"Who? Miss Kean? I should say I did. She was the life of the outdoor sketch club we got up; and believe me, she has a soul for color. Why, that little 'postage stamp landscape' she had in the American Artists' Exhibition was a winner. Did you see a memory sketch she did for the final exhibition at the League? It was a tall girl in black standing up singing and a beautiful red-headed girl in diaphanous blue playing an accompaniment on a guitar, with a background of holly and a great bunch of mistletoe at one side." Pierce stopped suddenly

18

in the midst of his description of Judy's picture and, gazing intently at Molly, cried out, "By the great jumping jingo, if Miss Brown isn't the red-headed girl in diaphanous blue!"

"Yes, I saw it," exclaimed Elise, "and thought it was wonderfully clever. Miss Kean got a splendid likeness of you, considering it was from memory."

"Oh, Judy has sketched me until she says doing me is almost as easy as writing her name. That must have been the Christmas party at Professor Green's when Melissa Hathaway was singing 'The Mistletoe Bough.' I remember Judy sat opposite us and I almost laughed out because she kept making pictures in the air with her thumb, which is a habit of hers when anything appeals to her as paintable. Won't it be splendid to see her again? Are you both going to Paris? You know Judy is there now and my mother and I are to join her."

"Glorious!" exclaimed the enthusiastic Pierce. "Of course I am going there; but how about you, Miss O'Brien?"

"Oh, I am to be there for a while, but my art is not considered seriously enough for me to stick at it long enough to accomplish much. Mother thinks Paris is nothing but one big shop, and when she has bought all the clothes we are supposed not to be able to be decent without, we have to go on. I am going to work while she shops. Thank goodness, she is so fussy that it takes her twice as long to get an outfit as it would anyone else, so I shall have time to get in some work," answered the girl bitterly.

Just then the gong was sounded for dinner. There was a general movement toward the saloon and the growing darkness prevented Molly from seeing the resentment on the face of Mrs. Huntington, if resentment she held, at the daughter's rudeness toward her.

"Such a nice girl," thought Molly, "and so clever and beautiful! But how, how can she be so horrid to her mother? There is no telling what provocation she has, though. Her mother was certainly not honest about the chairs; but then, your mother is your mother. Thank goodness, Aunt Clay is not mine!"

Molly hastened to her own mother's side and they made their way to the first meal on board.

CHAPTER III.

THE DEEP SEA.

Such a pleasant bustle, as the passengers came streaming into the cabin! Everyone seemed to have made or met some friend, with the exception of a few shy-looking, lonesome persons, and Molly devoutly hoped that these would find some congenial souls before very long and not be so forlorn. She and her mother had made such a fine beginning in the way of pleasant acquaintances that she wished the same good luck to all on board.

Their seats were next to the Captain, with Mr. Kinsella and Pierce opposite. The Captain was just what a captain ought to be: big and hearty, blond and bearded, with a booming laugh. "Like a Viking of old," whispered Molly to her mother.

"Good sailor, madam?" asked the Captain of Mrs. Brown.

"A Mississippi steamboat is the only test I have given myself so far, but my daughter and I are hoping we will prove good sailors," answered his neighbor. "We are evidently expected to be sick by our friends, as several of them have sent us remedies. Champagne from one, crystallized ginger from another and a box of big black pills from a third that look for all the world like shoe buttons."

"Well, don't trust to any of them. If you are sick, get on deck all you can and don't waste your champagne on seasickness, but get ginger ale, which is much cheaper and quite as effective," boomed the Captain with a laugh that made the glasses rattle.

Molly wished they would stop talking about seasickness! The food looked good. A plate of cream celery soup had just been placed in front of her. It seemed all that celery soup should be, but a qualm had suddenly arisen in her soul, (at least she called it her soul,) and she decided to let the soup go and wait for the next course.

"Uncle Tom, I have met an old friend of yours on board; also an acquaintance of my own from the Art Students' League," said Pierce as soon as the business of eating was well under way.

"Is that so? I'll bet on you for nosing around to find out things! Who is the gentleman?" inquired Mr. Kinsella.

"Gentleman much! It's a lady, and a very beautiful lady at that, who complimented you greatly by saying you looked like me," laughed the boy. "Her name is Mrs. Huntington."

"Huntington? I know no one of that name that I can remember. She must be some casual acquaintance who has slipped from my memory."

"Well, maybe,—anyhow, she called you Tom. Her daughter, Miss Elise O'Brien, is my friend."

Mr. Kinsella's face flushed and his somber eyes lit up with what Molly thought an angry light.

"So," he muttered, "she has married again. Yes, yes, my boy, I—I did know a Miss Lizzie Peck in my youth who married an old friend of mine, George O'Brien. I have not seen or heard of them for years and did not know George was dead. I shall take great pleasure in meeting his little girl."

"Little! She is as tall as Miss Brown, who is certainly not stumpy, and is some years older, if I am any judge of the fair sex."

"Of course you are a judge of the fair sex, a most competent one, I should say. What boy of eighteen is not?" teased his uncle. "Where are your new acquaintances seated?"

"They are at the other end of the next table with their backs to us. You will have to rubber a little to get a good view of them."

Mr. Kinsella accordingly "rubbered," as his slangy nephew put it, and satisfied himself of the identity of Mrs. Huntington. Molly was greatly interested in the occurrence. Mr. Kinsella was different from anyone she had ever seen before and Pierce's hint of a disappointed life had fired her imagination, ever ready for a romance. She had a feeling that the proud, beautiful, inconsiderate woman whose acquaintance she had recently made was in some way connected with Mr. Kinsella's disappointment.

Soup was removed and the next course of baked bluefish brought on. Molly's senses reeled and a drowsy numbness stole over her. "What a strange feeling! What on earth is the matter with me? I was so hungry when I came down here and now I can't touch a thing," she said to herself.

Mr. Kinsella was watching her and finally spoke:

"My dear Miss Brown, let me take you on deck. You will feel much better in the air."

"Why, my darling daughter, are you sick?" inquired the anxious mother, who was eating her dinner with the greatest enjoyment.

"I believe I'll go to bed," gasped poor Molly. "But don't you come, Mother. I'll be better in a minute."

A grim smile went down the Captain's table as Molly beat a hasty and ignominious retreat. Mrs. Huntington was heard to remark to her daughter as a white and hollow-eyed Molly flew past their chairs on the way to her stateroom: "There goes that red-headed girl from Kentucky, who was so rude to me on deck. I fancy we can occupy her chairs for a while longer."

"Oh, Mamma, why do we not have chairs of our own? It is so embarrassing to sponge on other people all the time, and the expense of chairs is not very great," implored Elise.

"Nonsense, Elise; I have crossed the ocean innumerable times and never get chairs. There are always enough seasick people who have to stay in their bunks, and since I abhor waste, I use their chairs. As you say, the expense is not very great, but if I do not save in small ways I cannot make ends meet and keep up appearances and that is most important, until you see fit to catch a husband."

All this was in an aside to her daughter, who seemed accustomed to such remarks and coolly helped herself to stuffed mangoes without deigning any reply. But after brooding a few seconds she spoke:

"Do you think that the chair episode on deck before dinner was 'keeping up appearances' very well?"

"And so you have your eye on young Mr. Kinsella, have you?"

"Not at all, Mamma, and you know I haven't. In the first place, Pierce Kinsella is years younger than I am, and while he is tremendously clever with his brush, he is not the intellectual man I must have or do without."

"Never mind your age. If you do not mind being frank on the subject, you must have some consideration for me, who am your unwilling mother. No one will ever believe I was a mere school girl when I married George O'Brien. If I should not keep up appearances for young Kinsella, who was it, please? Surely not that Miss Smith!"

"Miss Brown, Mamma, Molly Brown. She is a lovely girl and a perfect lady; and what will have more weight with you, she is a friend of the Stewarts. Pierce Kinsella told me it was at Mr. Stewart's request that she and her mother were put next to the Captain and they have the best stateroom the ship affords."

"Ah, dead-heads, I surmise."

"Not at all. They had their tickets and stateroom engaged and did not know of the honor done them until Pierce Kinsella told them himself. I fancy we are the only dead-heads on board."

"Elise, I will not have you be so cynical. Mr. Stewart is a connection of mine and I am entitled to some consideration from him," snapped the mother.

"Yes, I know, a very close connection: Mr. Huntington's first wife's cousin-in-law. For that reason, you must have transportation free on a line of steamers Mr. Stewart is interested in; but you had to send me to ask for the favor, and I'll tell you now what I did not tell you before for fear of hurting your feelings, that Mr. Stewart said he was glad to do it for my sake."

The last was a poser for the angry woman, and mother and daughter ceased their wrangling and devoted themselves to the very good dinner.

Poor Molly got to bed as best she could and stayed there twenty-four hours. She was sure her seasickness was the worst that had ever been known, but we all feel that. On the second day she was persuaded to go on deck by her solicitous mother,—who, by the way, was not uncomfortable one minute,—and as she dropped limply into her steamer chair, carefully arranged for her by the Kinsellas, she for the first time had a desire to live. The ocean was a wonderful color, all pearly gray with little flecks of pink on top of every wave. The sun was setting in a mist. The wind had died down and there was a delicious dampness in the air that smelt of salt.

"Oh, how glad I am to get up here! All of you are so good to me. It seems a year since I went to my stateroom and I believe it is only a day and a night. Has anything happened since I disappeared?"

"Nothing," answered Pierce. "The sun and the ship have moved but the rest of us have just stood still waiting for you to come back. By the way, this is your sunset, you remember. You forgot to advertise it, so you have not a very large audience."

"Well, if Miss Brown can get up that good a show without even trying, what couldn't she accomplish if she put her mind on it? I believe I like yours better than Pierce's," said Mr. Kinsella. "His was so flamboyant, while yours has a certain reserve and distinction."

The conversation went gayly on between uncle and nephew while Mrs. Brown hovered over her daughter, tucking in the rug and shifting the pillows for more perfect comfort. Molly smiled a little wanly at first but soon the good air and gay talk got in their perfect work, and before she knew it she was laughing outright at some of Pierce's sallies. The color began to come back into her cheeks. A desire for life grew stronger and stronger. Mr. Kinsella noticed the change in the girl, and while Mrs. Brown and Pierce were engaged in an animated discussion on Woman's Suffrage, Pierce taking the Anti side "just for practice," he slipped away and soon returned with a tray of dainty food.

"Please eat a little something now, Miss Brown. It will put new life in you and I feel sure you are on the mend and can trust yourself to take some nourishment. Chicken aspic and dry toast can't hurt you, and I feel sure it will do you good."

"Why, Mr. Kinsella, you are too good to me! How did you know I was hungry? I was ashamed to say so, but I felt that a little food was all that was needed to make me perfectly well." And Molly fell to with an avidity that surprised her mother, who had not been able to persuade her to take a mouthful all day.

"I have seen seasick persons before now," laughed Mr. Kinsella, "and know by experience that there is a crucial moment when food must be administered, and then the patient gets well immediately. I noticed you were laughing, and no one with *mal-de-mer* can laugh! And then your color came back, and that is a signal for food, too. I am so glad you like what I brought you."

"Mr. Kinsella, I cannot tell you how grateful I am," said Mrs. Brown. "I don't wish you to be seasick, but I do wish Molly and I could repay your kindness in some way."

"My dear lady, I am already in your debt for permitting my scape-grace nephew and me to know you and your daughter. I have had my nose at the grindstone of business for so many years that I feared it had grown out of my power to make new friends; but I begin to see that I have not lost the knack. Perhaps my somber presence is tolerated because of my gay, jolly boy," and Mr. Kinsella gazed rather wistfully after Pierce, who had crossed the deck to meet Elise O'Brien, just emerging from the cabin.

"Oh, Mr. Kinsella, you must not think that," eagerly implored Molly. "I always like serious men better than boys, and besides you are not somber but full of gaiety and jokes. You are not fair to yourself if you think people like you only on account of Pierce. He is a delightful boy, but——"

"But what?"

"Don't press her too far, Mr. Kinsella," laughed Mrs. Brown. "She has already confessed to a penchant to seriousness and finds 'beauty in extreme old age'," and pinching Molly's blushing cheek, she went over to join a group of recently made acquaintances who were looking at a distant sail through an overworked spyglass belonging to one of the tourists.

"What a tease Mother is! But she looks so like my brother Kent when she teases me that I don't mind. Kent is always teasing and the only reason I can stand it is that it makes him look like Mother! You see, Kent is my special beloved brother and you know what my mother is."

"Yes, I know," answered Mr. Kinsella, who had sunk into the chair vacated by Mrs. Brown. "Your mother is a rare woman: beautiful and honest and tolerant, charming and well-bred, broad-minded and cultured. Eternal youth is in her heart, but she has a character gracefully to accept the years that Providence has allotted her and that only serve to make her more lovely. I have no patience with the assumption of extreme youth in the middle-aged, despite the limerick I have taken for my motto."

"But, Mr. Kinsella, you are not middle-aged," protested Molly. "I never even think of Mother as being middle-aged. I think that is the ugliest word in our language, except, maybe, stout. I'd a great deal rather be called fat and forty than stout and middle-aged!"

"Well, it will be many a year before you will be called either, and by that time you may change your mind. 'A rose by any other name would smell as sweet,' and, after all, it is being stout and middle-aged that makes the difference, not being called it."

While Molly was having the little chat with Mr. Kinsella, Mrs. Huntington had come on deck and had approached them from behind. Looking up, Molly surprised on her face an expression of extreme bitterness, and she wondered if she had overheard Mr. Kinsella's views on the subject of the assumption of youth in the middle-aged. "I do hope she didn't," thought Molly. "She is so pretty, and it must be hard to give up youth and to feel your beauty slipping from you. Especially hard when beauty has been your chief asset in life, as I fancy it has been with Mrs. Huntington." She gave the older woman a polite bow and smile and Mr. Kinsella formally offered her his chair but with no great cordiality.

"Oh, thank you, Tom. And how are you, Miss Brown? I do hope you are feeling better. My daughter has taken such a fancy to you, she has been quite *désolé* at your nonappearance all day."

"Oh, I am all well again, thanks to Mr. Kinsella's getting me some food at the psychological moment when health was returning," answered Molly, wondering at Mrs. Huntington's change of tactics since the evening before, when she had been so insolent in her bearing to her. "It is certainly nicer to have her polite to me than rude, whether she means it or not," she said to herself. "I do wish I had not been sick all day. I did want to see her first meeting with Mr. Kinsella. I know she had something to do with his premature grayness and the disappointment that Pierce hinted at. How coldly polite he is to her now. If a man like that had ever loved me and then could be so cold to me, I believe it would kill me," which shows that Molly was very sentimental and on the lookout for romance.

The gong rang for dinner and there was a general move toward the cabin.

"Please tell Mother I am all right and will sit here while she is at dinner, and that she must not hurry. I believe 'discretion would be the better part of valor' for me and I had better not try to eat anything more for a while."

After the deck was clear except for a few helplessly, hopelessly sick persons who lay like mummies in their chairs, ranged along the deck, Molly decided to get up and walk around a little, feeling anxious to try her sea legs. Then as the wind had shifted, she determined to move her chair to a sheltered nook behind one of the life-boats. She bundled herself up in her rug, pulling the corner of it over her head and lay for all the world like the rest of the mummies. "Only, thank goodness, I am no longer sick," she thought gratefully.

Her soul was at peace, after the night and day of agony, and she dropped off easily into a doze. She dreamed that she was at home in the old apple tree that they had called "The Castle" and that Kent was gently shaking the tree, trying to make her get out so Professor Green could build his bungalow there; and when she refused and declared it was her Castle and she intended to stay in it, the Professor himself had come, with his kind brown eyes looking into hers, and said: "But, Miss Molly, the bungalow is yours, too, and the Orchard is still your home." She awoke but lay quite still wondering at the reality of her dream.

CHAPTER IV.

WHAT MOLLY OVERHEARD.

It had grown quite dark. The passengers were evidently still at dinner. A man loomed up close to her and then stopped, evidently unaware of her presence. Leaning over the rail and gazing into the black depths of water, he emitted a sigh that seemed to come from his soul. Suddenly a woman joined him. Molly was still half asleep, thinking of the orchard at Chatsworth and of what Professor Green's bungalow would look like among the apple trees. Her thoughts came back to the ship with a bounce when she heard the woman say:

"Tom, why do you avoid me? Can't you let bygones be bygones?"

"That is exactly what I am doing, Mrs. Huntington: letting bygones be bygones. It seems a useless thing for us to rake up the past."

"'Mrs. Huntington' sounds very cold and formal coming from your lips."

"Well, I gathered you did not think much of the name of Lizzie since you have changed your daughter's to Elise."

"Oh, Tom, you are cruel!"

"Now see here, Mrs. Huntington, I do not want to be rude to you. I have lived in total ignorance of you and your affairs for twenty-five years, and since by chance we meet on a steamer, you cannot make me feel that what I do or say is of the slightest importance to you. You made the young Tom Kinsella about as miserable as a man could be, but the old Tom is immune from misery, thank God, and there is no use in trying to get a flame from the dead ashes of the past. I am very glad to see you again and especially glad to make the acquaintance of the daughter of my old friend, George O'Brien."

"You forgive George but do not forgive me."

"I have nothing to forgive George, and you know it. He was the soul of honor and had no idea of there being an engagement between us, when he married you. I am as sure of this as though George himself had told me. In those good old days in Paris when we were all of us art students, George and I were great chums. I could read him like a book and there never lived a more honest fellow.

"When my father died and his foundry at Newark seemed in a fair way to be on its last legs for want of management and the family income was in danger of being decidedly lessened, you persuaded me, in fact, you put it up to me, to give you up or give up art and go to work and pull the foundry out of the hole.

"Art meant a lot to me, but at the time you meant a lot more. You remember you would not let me announce our engagement to our friends, not even to George.

"I went back to America and piled into a work, entirely uncongenial, but determined to win out. Things were in an awful mess because of my father's long inability to attend to business. My brother Pierce was still in college and could be of no assistance to me. I had to master the business from the beginning, learning every detail before I could put it on the efficiency basis that I knew it must attain before I could be satisfied.

"I wrote you rather discouraged letters, I will admit, but I felt I could pour out my soul to you and you alone. I knew it would be two or three years before it would be expedient for us to marry, but my faith in you was supreme and it never entered my head you would not wait for me.

"When the goal was in sight, you may imagine the shock it gave me when a casual acquaintance, recently returned from Paris, spoke of having had such a gay time at your wedding breakfast, given in old George's studio (the one I used to share with him) by his fellow students.

"Not a word from you; later on a letter from George, full of happiness and your charms and explaining to me how it came about he could marry. He had been one of the poorest among a lot of fellows, where poverty was the rule and not the exception; but his uncle, the Brooklyn politician, had died and left him a hundred thousand dollars. That seemed immense wealth to the Latin Quarter, and there was rejoicing in all of the ateliers where George O'Brien was a general favorite and Lizzie Peck was known as the prettiest American girl in the Quarter.

"The shock was so great I was like a dead man for weeks, but I never told a soul of my pitiful love affair. I got over the loss of you as soon as I could pull myself together enough to think that if you were the kind who could do as you did, I was well out of it; and George had my pity and not my envy. But my Art—my Art—nothing can ever make up to me for giving it up. I could not go back to it, as I had plunged too deeply into the foundry affairs to pull out, and one cannot serve business and Art at the same time. Art is too jealous a mistress to share her lover's time with anything else. I went on with the work and came out very well.

"This is the first real holiday I have had for many years, but I am determined to have a good time and am not going to let regret prey upon me."

Molly had been a forced listener to this long speech, but she could not fool herself into thinking she had been an unwilling one. She was thrilled to the soul by Mr. Kinsella's history. No wonder he was so sad looking and occasionally so bitter! She was glad he had not truckled to the spoiled Mrs. Huntington, but had let her know exactly where he stood. It was not so very chivalrous of him, but she needed a good mental and moral slap and Mr. Kinsella had administered it as gently as possible, no doubt.

What was Molly to do now? To let them know she was there would make it horribly embarrassing for all concerned, and still she felt she had already heard more than she had any business to know.

"I'll have to pretend I am asleep and never divulge to a soul, (except Mother, of course,) that I have overheard this tremendously interesting conversation."

Mrs. Huntington was silenced for a few moments by Mr. Kinsella's harangue, but finally spoke:

"Tom, you are hard on me. I was very young at the time and had always been so poor."

"That is so, Lizzie. It was hard on you to be so poor; but you were not so very young. You must have been about the age your daughter is now, and I fancy you would not excuse much in her because of her youth. You were two years older than I was in those days."

"Brute!"

"Mind you, I said 'in those days.' I do not mean you are still two years older than I am."

Molly was sorry that Mr. Kinsella was pushing the poor lady so far. She made a quick calculation from the evidence in hand and realized that Mrs. Huntington must be about forty-nine. "Almost as old as Mother! And just look at her hair and clothes! She looks much younger, and I know it is hard on her to give up her youth. I do wish Mr. Kinsella had not said that to her about being two years older than he is! It was not very kind, even if she did jilt him. It seems a small revenge to me. I wish I could have made my presence known and then I should not have heard Mr. Kinsella belittle himself, which I certainly think he did."

Poor Mrs. Huntington swallowed her resentment as best she could and continued the conversation: "There is one thing I should like to ask of you as a favor, Tom, and that is: please do not tell Elise that her father and I ever studied art. Not that I ever studied very hard, but George was certainly much interested and it took a deal of managing to persuade him to give it up and go into politics. You see, his uncle's influence was still hot and there were many plums waiting for him. I was too ignorant in those days to know that it did not necessarily follow that political jobs brought social success.

"George was very successful and doubled his inheritance, but we had no position at all. He changed a great deal. You would hardly have known him in his last years. You remember how gay and light-hearted and good-tempered he always was. Well, he lost it all and became morose and bitter. Elise was the only person who had any influence on him at all. We had to live in Brooklyn and how I did hate it!"

"How long has George been dead?"

"Oh, ten years or so. Elise was a mere child and George never spoke to her of having wished to become an artist. It seemed best to me for her to live in ignorance of the fact as she is already ridiculously fond of trying to paint; and if she knew there were any hereditary reasons for it, there is no telling what stand she would take. I hate the Bohemian life that artists lead, and now that I have made so many sacrifices for her to place her in the best society, I have no idea of allowing her to drop out.

"We are received in the most exclusive houses in New York and Newport, and while our means do not permit us to entertain very largely, our at-homes are most popular with the Four Hundred.

"Elise is very stubborn. She has had several excellent offers but refuses to consider anyone whom she does not love. George O'Brien was very sentimental and she has inherited that from him, along with her love for dabbling."

Mr. Kinsella had maintained a grim silence during this heartless speech; but he now asked: "What sacrifice have you made for your daughter's welfare, you poor put-upon lady?"

"Why, I married Ponsonby Huntington! He had not a *sou* to his name but he had the *entrée* into all the fashionable homes in the East. He was a great expense, but it fully repaid me, as he lived long enough to establish Elise and me in that society for which we are eminently fitted. I am deeply grateful to him and his family and do not begrudge the money, now that he is dead.

"I was keen enough not to let him go into my principal very largely. I am an excellent business woman, Tom, and have managed my affairs wonderfully well."

"So it seems," muttered Mr. Kinsella. "You have evidently satisfied all your ideals. I am glad to tell you that I have already divulged to Elise that her father might have become a very good painter, and

34

was astonished that she was ignorant of the fact that he had ever drawn a line in his life. I say that I am glad, as I want to talk to George's daughter about her father, and I cannot think of my old friend, George O'Brien, as anything but the gay, care-free art student, always ready to go on a lark and to share his last penny, of which he had very few, with any needy fellow-student. Don't you ever feel like painting yourself?"

"No! I hate the sight of a paint brush, and as for adding in any way to the ever-increasing flood of poorly painted pictures, —I can at least claim my innocence of that crime."

"Perhaps you are right, but you used to be so clever at catching a likeness."

"Elise has the same power, but I hate to see it in her and never encourage her by the least praise. Of course you can't understand this feeling, but I know the girl would fly off at the slightest chance and live in that shabby Latin Quarter. There, no doubt, she would marry some down-at-the-heel artist, who would live on her money and go on painting bad pictures to the end of time; and she would aid and abet him and paint worse ones herself!"

"Elise has money, then?"

"The money is all hers except my pitiful third that the law allows me, and I had to go into that a little to keep Ponsonby Huntington in a good humor. However, Elise cannot get control of her money until she is twenty-five and I have several years yet. She is quite equal to throwing me over in spite of all I have done for her." Mrs. Huntington spoke with a rancor that was really astounding to Molly, whose own mother was so different that the girl had an idea that all mothers must have some of Mrs. Brown's qualities.

"Oh, I am sure you are mistaken in judging your daughter thus severely! She must have inherited from George some other traits along with the artistic talent."

"That is just it. She inherited from him this very tendency to be hard on me. Was it kind or right for George to leave all the money to her; and to me, his devoted and long-suffering wife, nothing more than the law exacted? My only hope is that she may marry a man rich enough to make a handsome settlement on me. One who will have money enough not to regard Elise's fortune at all, except, perhaps, to realize the necessity of turning it over to me. Now tell me: do you think the Latin Quarter a likely place for a girl to find such a husband?"

"Oh, I don't know. You did pretty well there, and if you had waited for me, you might have done even better from a financial standpoint, as I have been very successful as the world takes it. Perhaps poor little Elise might have equal luck. Oh, Lizzie, Lizzie, how changed you are! You have spoken only of money and position and society; never once of love and humanity. I can't bear to see you this way. When I think of you as a girl with your soft, sweet manner and no more worldliness than a kitten, I can hardly bear to contemplate this change in you."

"Oh la, la, Tom, you and I know that a kitten only takes a year to grow into a horrid cat, and as you so brutally and frankly put it, I have had about twenty-five years to grow and sharpen my claws. You struck this note first in our conversation. I was prepared to be as nice as you once thought me, but I saw how cynical you had grown and I knew there was no use in putting on; so I have rather enjoyed showing you my true self. Anyhow, you are grateful to me for throwing you over, now that you see what I am. Is it not so?"

Mr. Kinsella did not answer for a moment, but finally said, changing the subject: "There is one thing I am going to ask of you for auld lang syne and I think maybe you will grant it: let Elise put in this winter in a good studio in Paris. She is hungry for a long period of uninterrupted work and I know it will soften her toward you instead of hardening her; and I feel sure that when the dreaded twenty-fifth birthday arrives, she will want to settle half of the fortune on you. Do this for me, Lizzie. I guarantee it will come out well for you."

Mrs. Huntington hesitated for a moment and then by a quick calculation came to the conclusion that it would be a good thing, after all, and would leave her free to go where she chose. She well knew how cheaply a girl could board in Paris when she was at work in a studio, and, as Tom said, there was every chance of her picking up a rich husband among the students. There were always some young men who were rolling in wealth, but still had the artistic bee in their bonnets.

"I'll do it, Tom, but if it turns out badly I'll have you to thank."

"Lizzie, now you are more like your old self and I am grateful to you for this concession. Come, let us find Elise and tell her the good news."

Molly was indeed glad to have the interview over. It was against her whole honest nature to eavesdrop, but she felt it best for all concerned for her to remain quiet. As soon as Mr. Kinsella and Mrs. Huntington had disappeared, Molly beat a hasty retreat to her stateroom where her mother was looking for her, not being able to find her on deck.

"Oh, Mother, I am so excited!" And she told Mrs. Brown all about her forced concealment during the intimate conversation between the old lovers.

"It is very interesting, certainly, and I hardly know how you could help being a listener. Since it will go no farther, as of course neither of us will ever mention the matter to a soul, it will do no harm. I wish you had not had to hear it, however, as I hate for my Molly to realize that such women as Mrs. Huntington exist, so cold and selfish and worldly. I am glad poor Elise is to be allowed to stay in Paris all winter and work. Perhaps we can make up to her some for her mother's heartlessness."

So mother and daughter kissed and went to bed; Molly waked the next morning with no trace of seasickness, ready and eager to enjoy the rest of the voyage.

The trip was delightful to both mother and daughter. They made many acquaintances on board, but Elise O'Brien and the two Kinsellas they counted among their real friends. So closely were the five thrown together on the voyage, that they often said it seemed as though they had known one another all their lives. Mrs. Huntington kept to herself much of the time. She seemed to realize that it was policy to let Elise have as good a time as she could with her father's old friend and his nephew; and since the Browns seemed to have influential and wealthy friends, they could, at least, do her daughter no harm, and might even prove useful during the girl's sojourn in Paris.

Elise bloomed in this congenial atmosphere and did not look like the same girl. She had a ready wit, was quick at repartee, and after a while her tongue lost its bitterness and her sarcastic humor became much more genial.

Mr. Kinsella would often say: "That is like your father. He had the kindest humor in the world and was truly Irish in his wit." But when she was too critical or inclined to let her wit run away with her heart, he would shake his head and look sad; and the girl began to care what her father's friend thought of her, and tried to please him.

She had liked Molly from the minute they clasped hands when Pierce introduced them, and this liking grew to enthusiastic love. She had had few intimates and this friendship was wonderful to her. Mr. Kinsella realized the importance of this wholesome influence on his charge, (he had made Elise his charge ever since he wrung from her mother the promise to let her continue her studies in art), and he did everything to throw the girls together and give them opportunities to talk their eager girls' talk.

"I hate to think of the journey coming to an end," said Molly. "It has been splendid; but if the trip is nearly over, our friendship has just begun! And what times we can have in Paris! Isn't it great that you and Judy know each other and that the three of us are so congenial?"

Elise looked sad. "Yes, it is fine, but I know you and Judy will want me out of the way. You are such old friends, and I shall always feel like an interloper."

"Oh, Elise, Elise! You must not feel that way for an instant. Judy and I love each other a whole lot, but we are not a bit inclined to pair off and not make new friends. Judy is more than likely already to have begun a big affair of friendship with somebody. She will get so thick with that one that she will have no time for anyone else; and then she will find out the person is not the paragon she had imagined and come weeping back to me," said Molly, throwing her arm around Elise and giving her a warm hug.

"Well, let's enjoy the few hours left to us. It seems hardly possible that this is the same, stupid old boat that we boarded a little over a week ago. I hated it, our stuffy stateroom, the crowded table; and then I always dread a long voyage with Mamma. She gets so cross and overbearing when she is cut off from society and amusements and ——" Elise stopped suddenly. She felt Molly's friendly arm growing slack around her waist and she realized that her new friends, the Browns, could not tolerate her impertinent remarks to and about her mother. "Oh, Molly, please excuse me. I am trying to be nicer about Mamma. It is awfully ill-bred of me to speak of her in that way, no matter how I feel."

"Elise, why don't you try to feel differently and then it would be impossible for you to speak so?"

"Oh, Molly, I will try." And it shows she was already trying, for she did not add what was in her heart to say, "If you only knew my mother you would not ask that of me."

CHAPTER V.

PARIS.

"Judy! Judy! I can't believe that we are really here, that this is Paris, and that you are you! As for me, I feel like 'there was an old woman as I've heard tell' who said 'Lawk a mercy on me, this surely can't be I.'"

Molly settled herself with a sigh of supreme enjoyment on the lumpy seat of an extremely rickety taxi that Judy had engaged to take the Browns from the station to Mrs. Pace's very exclusive pension on the Boulevard St. Michel.

"It does seem almost too good to be true that I have got you and your dear mother at last. I have not been able to work for a week because of the excitement of expectation. I went over to Monroe's this morning and got your mail. I could hardly lug it home, both of you had such a batch. You see, the mail has beaten your slow steamer in and everyone is writing to have a greeting ready for you in Paris." And Judy, who was in the middle, put embracing arms around both Mrs. Brown and Molly as they rode down the Avenue de l'Opera.

How wonderful Paris looked to them on that clear, crisp day in autumn! She was showing her best and most smiling aspect to the travelers, which delighted Judy, as she felt quite responsible for her beloved city and wanted her friends to like it as much as she did. They passed various points of interest which Judy pointed out with pride, and which brought answering thrills from Mrs. Brown and Molly.

The streets were gay with little pushcarts, laden with chrysanthemums and attended by the most delightful looking old women. Everyone seemed to be in a good humor and no one in much of a hurry except the chauffeurs, and they went whizzing by at a most incredible speed through the crowded thoroughfares.

"How clean the streets are!" exclaimed Mrs. Brown. "And what a good smell!"

"Oh, I just wondered if you would notice the smell! That is Paris. 'Every city has an odor of its own,' Papa says, and I believe he is right. Paris smells better than New York, although I like the smell in New York, too; but Paris has a strange freshness in its odor that reminds me of flowers and good things to eat, and suggests gay times, rollicking fun and adventure."

"Same old Judy," laughed Molly, "with her imagination on tap."

Just then they ran under the arches of the Louvre into the Place du Carrousel, and Molly held her breath with wonder and delight. Then came the Seine with its beautiful bridges, its innumerable boats, and its quays with the historic secondhand book stalls where Edwin Green had looked forward to walking with her, searching for treasures of first editions and what not. "Never mind," thought Molly, "Professor Green may come later and the first editions will keep."

"There is the wonderful statue of Voltaire, and through this street you can catch a glimpse of the Beaux Arts," chanted Judy. "Now look out, for before you know it we will be in the aristocratic Faubourg St. Germain, — and then the Luxembourg Gardens, — and here we are at our own respectable door before we are ready for it! Now Mrs. Pace will eat both of you up for a while and I cannot get a word in edgewise."

The Pension Pace was on the corner where a small street ran into the broad boulevard at a sharp angle, making the building wedge-shaped. It was a very imposing looking house and Mrs. Brown wondered at a woman being able to conduct such a huge affair. She expressed her surprise to Judy, who informed her that Mrs. Pace had only the three upper floors and that the other flats were let to different tenants.

"The elevator takes us to the fifth floor, where Mrs. Pace has her parlors, dining salon and swellest boarders, — at least the boarders able to pay the most. Of course *we* do not think that they are the swellest, since we are on the seventh floor ourselves. Who so truly swell as we?" Judy got out of the taxi with such an assumption of great style that the chauffeur, much impressed, demanded a larger *pourboire* than she saw fit to give him.

"They always try to make you pay more, no matter what you offer. I am adamant, however, where cabbies and chauffeurs are concerned. Papa says, 'Look after the tips and the legitimate expenses will look after themselves.' So I look after the tips and trust to luck for the rest to come out right. I am not much of an economist, I fear, but I am learning, now that I am on a strict allowance."

An elevator, so slow that its progress was almost imperceptible, took them to the fifth floor where Mrs. Pace was in readiness to receive them. Her greeting was very cordial and condescending. She seemed to be taking them under her protecting wing, giving them to understand that with her they had nothing more to fear or worry about; and as Molly and her mother had nothing in particular to worry about and certainly nothing to fear, they were very much amused by her attitude toward them. Judy was purple with suppressed merriment as Mrs. Pace advised them to go right to bed, to rest up from their long journey, poor sick, miserable, friendless females.

Mrs. Brown assured her that she was not at all tired and never felt better in her life; that she had made many friends on the steamer; and that she would freshen up a bit with some soap and water and then go out for a walk with Miss Julia Kean. Mrs. Brown had reckoned without her host, however, as the intrepid Mrs. Pace took them to their room on the seventh floor, just across the hall from Judy's, and did not leave them until they were in their kimonos and actually lying down.

"You must not try to keep up, dear ladies, when you are overfatigued and ill. Bed is the best place for you, bed and quiet. Miss Kean had better leave you now and let you have a little nap."

While Mrs. Pace talked, she had plumped up their pillows and lowered the shade of the one large window, opened their suitcases and got out their kimonos and, despite their feeble protest, had actually undressed them and put them to bed! Then, forcibly ejecting Judy, she shut the door with admonitions for them to sleep until dinner at six-thirty.

Judy went very dutifully to her room until she heard the last of Mrs. Pace's ponderous tread on the stairs; then she crept softly to the Browns' door and gently opened it to find Mrs. Brown and Molly rolling on the bed, overcome with laughter.

"Oh, oh, oh! She has taken at least forty-five years off of my age," giggled Mrs. Brown like a veritable boarding-school miss. "I have never in my life seen such a born boss as the redoubtable Mrs. Pace! Did you see her undo my belt and take off my skirt? I could not have felt more like a child if my waist had been a pinafore instead of a respectable black silk. And as for Molly, she was treated as though she were just about old enough to go into rompers." And they all went off into peals of laughter.

"Well, now is the time to take a stand or you will never be able to," said Judy. "I defied her from the first and she lets me alone wonderfully."

"Yes, I noticed how you withstood her authority when you were sent to your room!" grinned Molly, as she got back into the clothes that had been forcibly removed only five minutes before. "I see you have sneaked in our letters and I, for one, am going to read mine, and then if we can get down stairs without the dragon devouring us, let's take a walk. We shall have plenty of time before dinner."

They accordingly read their letters and crept down stairs and out on the street for a breath of air and a stroll in the Luxembourg Gardens. It was too late to try to see the pictures in the Gallery of the Luxembourg and, after all, they had the winter before them. And now that she was out on the street, having escaped the dragon, Mrs. Brown confessed to feeling a little mite tired, so they sat down on a bench in the Gardens and watched the children play.

"Poor Mrs. Brown, of course you are tired! That is the most irritating thing about Mrs. Pace: she is always right. 'It is best to rest after a trip whether you feel tired or not, as the reaction after a journey is obliged to come, and you pay up for it to-morrow if you do not rest to-day'," and Judy imitated Mrs. Pace to the life.

"Well, you may be sure, my dear girls, that wild horses will not drag the fact from me in the presence of the dragon, even if I am weary unto death. Does she coerce all her boarders as she did me, Judy?"

"Most of them are completely under her dominion, finding it easiest and best to take the course of least resistance. Some few rebel, but they usually end by moving on. If you stay at the Pension Pace and wish to *"requiescat in pace,"* you do as she says to do. I have defied her from the first and now I am rated as an undesirable boarder. Had it not been that she was wild to have you with her because of your relationship to the Marquise d'Ochtè, she would have raised some cock and bull story about my room having been engaged by someone a year ago and, since her honor was at stake, she would have to ask me to vacate.

"I tell you she is a sly one. You must either have lots and loads of money, or you must do as she says, do—or die. Of course she has an excellent house in a most desirable quarter and she caters to Americans. You will notice that the food is much more American than French; and after people have been knocking around the Continent, of course they are overjoyed to have some food that seems like home."

"But I don't want American food," wailed Molly. "I want French things, even snails; and I want to learn how to ask for these things in the most Frenchy style. What is the use in coming to Paris and staying with a stuffy old dame from Philadelphia and eating the things we have at home?"

"Oh, I am so glad you feel that way! How about you, Mrs. Brown? Papa and Mamma made me promise to do just as you thought best. They put me in Mrs. Pace's house and I have been determined not to worry them about changing, but I am 'most dead of her and her ways. Do say you think we ought to go to housekeeping or should get in a French family; anything to get out of the dragon's den," pleaded Judy.

"For how long did you engage our room?" asked Mrs. Brown, smiling at Judy's despair.

"One week; and mine, also, is taken by the week. She tried to make Papa sign for the whole winter, but he was on to her from the first and refused to do more than take it from week to week. He and Mamma stayed here a few days on their way to Turkey, and you would have died laughing if you had seen Mrs. Pace try to make Papa 'Fletcherize.' You know he always eats as though the train would not wait. At every meal she remarked on it and one day said at dinner: 'This is veal, Mr. Kean, and should be thoroughly masticated.' Whereupon he put down his knife and fork and, looking her solemnly in the eye, said: 'That is good advice no doubt for ordinary mortals, but after long years in railroad camps I have acquired a gizzard.' With that he took a great piece of *blanquette de veau* and to all appearances swallowed it whole without changing his expression. I choked so I had to leave the table and I believe Mrs. Pace, to this day, thinks that by a skillful legerdemain I swallowed the veal! Anyhow, Bobby ate to suit himself after that."

"Oh, Judy, how ridiculous you are! I wish I could have seen Mr. Kean execute his daring feat," laughed Molly. "Mother, let's look around for an apartment and go to housekeeping immediately. I am sorry we told Elise O'Brien about Mrs. Pace's. I can't bear for her to be anywhere that is not pleasant. She has had tribulations enough in her day."

Judy had not yet heard anything of their fellow passengers, as they had been so occupied with Paris and the pension that they had had no time to tell her of their voyage and the pleasant people they had met. She was much interested in the fact that Miss O'Brien was to be at the art school for the winter and said she was a girl of undoubted talent. As for young Kinsella, he was the cleverest draughtsman at the League.

"Do you girls think you like Elise enough to have her come to live with us for the winter?" asked Mrs. Brown. "I feel sure the poor girl would be happy, and if you would all fit in together and be congenial, I really think it would be an act of charity to ask her. We must consider it from all sides before we rush into it, however."

"Mother, it would be splendid!" declared Molly. "I believe Mrs. Huntington was dying for you to ask Elise, but of course had to wait for you to suggest it. We could divide the expenses into four parts and I know it would be cheaper than boarding and infinitely more agreeable."

"Mrs. Brown, I am sure we should get on like a house afire, and it does seem as though we might take Elise in and give her a pleasant home. I promise to be real good and get on with everybody, if I can only know I am to leave the *Maison Pace* in peace," promised Judy.

So it was decided by these three impulsive souls to take in Elise O'Brien and to get a flat forthwith and leave the sheltering wing of the dragon. Mrs. Brown thought it best to stay a fortnight in their present quarters so they could look well about them; she also wanted to see her old friend and cousin, the Marquise d'Ochtè, for if she were anything like the Sally Bolling of old, she felt sure she could depend on her for some assistance in the matter of getting settled.

"Of course, she may have changed so, after being married to a French nobleman for some twenty-eight years, that I will hesitate to ask anything of her; but I have an idea old Sally could not change. I remember her as being a great harum-scarum but with the best heart in the world, and absolutely honest and unaffected. My experience is that honest, unaffected people do not change in the long run."

"What did she look like, Mother?" asked Molly.

"Well, when I come to think of it, she looked a little like you. She is only my second cousin, once removed, not such very close kin; but this red hair of yours comes cropping out in every generation or so in my family and the similar coloring makes one fancy a likeness even if there is none; but Sally had your eyes and your chin. She took life much more lightly than my Molly does, saw a jest where none was intended and sometimes cracked a joke when seriousness would have been in better taste. I have not seen her for many years and she stopped corresponding with all of us; not that there was any disagreement, but letter-writing simply died a natural death, as time went on. I am greatly interested in seeing her."

Mrs. Brown also decided to let Mr. Kinsella approach the O'Briens in regard to having Elise live with her. She was very well aware of Mrs. Huntington's nature and felt that that lady would be fully capable of treating her as though Elise were necessary to the housekeeping scheme to help out the financial end; and Mrs. Brown was determined to have no one with her as a boarder, but to run the *ménage* on a co-operative principle, letting all of them share the expense.

Mrs. Huntington and Elise had stopped in Brussels for a visit with some friends and Mr. Kinsella and Pierce were still in Antwerp getting their fill of the pictures to be seen there. They were uncertain how long it would take them to grow tired of the interesting Belgian city and could not tell just when their friends might expect them in Paris.

When the three renegades returned from their walk in the Luxembourg Gardens, they hoped to reach their rooms without being seen by Mrs. Pace, but that lady's motto was "Eternal Vigilance," and no one went out of her house or came in unobserved. She met them as they stepped off the elevator on the fifth floor and gently but firmly admonished them for their disobedience. Molly noticed her mother's heightening color and her quivering nostrils and remembered with a smile what Aunt Mary, their old cook, always said to them when they were children: "Ole Miss is long suffrin' an' slow to anger but when her nose gits to wuckin', you chillun ought to learn that she done had 'nuf and you had better make yo'sefs scurse." Peace-loving Molly drew Mrs. Brown's arm through her own and gently pressing it, led her upstairs.

"Thank you, my dear, I was on the verge of attacking the dragon, and since we are to be here two weeks, I must not do anything to make it more difficult. But did you ever see anyone more impertinent?" asked Mrs. Brown, still sniffing the battle from afar.

"Never," sympathized Judy. "I wish you had said your say. I believe you could get ahead of the fabulous monster in open combat. She is, after all, a very flabby, fabulous monster and one prick would do for her."

CHAPTER VI.

LA MARQUISE.

"*La Marquise d'Ochtè* is attending *Madame Brune* in the *salon au cinquième étage*," announced a very excited little housemaid, who was supposed to speak English for the benefit of the American pensionnaires at *Maison Pace*. "*Madame Pace* is some time gone at the *boucher*, not expecting callers at so early *heur*. *La Marquise* demanded not *Madame Pace*; but said very *distinctment* '*Madame Brune et sa fille*'."

"Very well, Alphonsine, thank you so much. My daughter and I will come down immediately," said Mrs. Brown, smiling at the agitation of the little maid. Mrs. Pace had evidently given her servants to understand the importance her pension gained from the visits of a marchioness.

"Milly, Milly, how I have longed to see you," and the Marquise d'Ochtè rose from her seat and clasped her one-time friend and beloved cousin in a warm embrace. "And this is your daughter? Goodness, child, you look like me,—at least, like me when I was young!"

Molly knew in the first second of greeting that she was going to like this cousin, and Mrs. Brown was delighted to see in the marchioness the same Sally Bolling of thirty years ago. She was like Molly in a way, but it was hard to realize that Molly could ever be quite so buxom as this middle-aged cousin. She was a very large woman with an excellent figure for her weight, and hair a little darker than Molly's with no silver threads showing so far.

"I pull 'em out if they dare to so much as show their noses. They say forty will come in when you pull out one, but then I'll make my maid pull out forty, if it kills me in the pulling," she declared when Mrs. Brown remarked on it in the course of their inventory of each other. "My Jean declares he got caught in my hair and could not get away, and I mean still to keep him."

"I am afraid I would snatch myself bald-headed if I tried to pull all of my gray hairs out," laughed Mrs. Brown; "but, Sally, you are exactly the same girl who left Kentucky ages ago; there is just a little more of you."

"A little more of me, indeed! There is about twice as much of me as there used to be. But, Milly, you are exactly the same; there is not even any more of you. You look much more like a member of the French nobility than I do."

The marchioness did not look in the least French, but more like a well-groomed English woman. Her dark brown suit was very simple and well made, and her shoes bore the earmarks of an English boot maker, fitting her perfectly but with low heels, broad toes and heavy soles. Her hat was the only French touch about her, and that could have been concocted in no spot in the world but Paris, so perfectly did it blend with her hair and furs.

"Now tell me all about yourselves and what you are going to do with your winter, and we can 'reminisce' another time. We must hurry before Henny Pace gets back from market. I came early so as to avoid her and see you a moment alone. She is a kind, good soul and I am really very fond of her for auld lang syne, but you might as well try to hold a conversation with a bumping bug in the room as Henrietta. Firstly, do you mean to stay here?"

Molly and her mother laughed outright at the bumping bug comparison. It was very apt.

"Why, Cousin Sally, we could not think of spending the winter being coerced at every turn," returned Molly. "We were hardly in the house before Mrs. Pace actually took Mother's clothes off and put her to bed, and last night at dinner she refused to let me have any coffee. She said it would ruin my complexion!"

The marchioness roared with laughter. "How like old Henny that is! She always was a boss, but I don't blame you for objecting. I let her seem to boss me just for the fun of it. I have known her since first coming to Paris and understand how good she is at bottom, but wild horses could not drag me to spend a night in her house. I ask her to

49

la Roche Craie every year and try to give her a rest, (she really works awfully hard,) but she is so busy there trying to change my housekeeper's methods and rearrange the linen presses that she gets very little rest after all. Jean cannot stand her, but my son Philippe sees the good in her that I have brought him up to see; and then he clings to any and everything American. I am anxious for you to know my husband and son and for them to meet you. Do you know French?"

"Mother speaks better French than I do in spite of my work at college," confessed Molly.

"Well, I studied French with the old time method more as we study Latin, and while my accent is vile, my verbs are all right. I am going to try to brace up in accent, and Molly and Judy are endeavoring to perfect themselves in grammar. But you have not met our friend Judy, Miss Julia Kean," said Mrs. Brown.

"No, I have not, but from all the complaints Henny Pace has made of her, I know she must be charming. When Henny gives a boarder a good character, I know without meeting her that she is some spineless old maid who is afraid to call her soul her own, or that she is a hypocrite like me who wants peace at any price. Now she tells me that Miss Kean is head-strong, self-willed, flippant, slangy, ill-bred, inconsiderate——"

"Oh, how could she tell such things?" interrupted Molly. "Why, Cousin Sally, Judy is splendid! She is independent and knows her own mind, and all of us are a little slangy, I am afraid; but she is very well-bred and Mother says the most considerate visitor she has ever had."

"Well, child, her report of your friend had no effect on me but to make me want to meet the young lady, so I can judge for myself. I want you and your mother to come and dine with us this evening at six-thirty and to bring Miss Kean with you. We will go to the opera to hear *Louise*. It is wonderful and I know you will like it," and la Marquise d'Ochtè smiled on her young Kentucky cousin and pressed her hand, pleased to see how she could speak up for her friend.

"We shall be delighted to come," said Mrs. Brown, "and I know Judy will appeal to you. She is a dear child and as free from affectation as you yourself. Now, Sally, tell me how we must go to work to find an apartment and where we should settle ourselves. We are far from affluent and want something inexpensive but, of course, respectable. Judy is to be with us; also a Miss Elise O'Brien, whose acquaintance we made on the steamer. You know so many persons, I wonder if you ever met her mother: she was a Miss Lizzie Peck, who married a young artist, George O'Brien, some twenty-five years ago here in Paris. At his death she married Mr. Huntington."

"Know Lizzie Peck? I should say I did,—the outrageous piece! You see, before Jean succeeded to the estate and before I had my windfall from Aunt Sarah Carmichael, we lived in a very small way and our principal society was in Bohemia. At that time Lizzie Peck was the beauty of the Latin Quarter. She was supposed to be studying art, and indeed she was quite clever. But she was such a belle and so busy drawing young men to her, that she did not give much time to any other drawing. George O'Brien was much too good for her in every way. He was one of the wittiest men I ever knew and good nature itself. It is to be hoped that the daughter Elise inherited a disposition from him and not from the flirtatious Lizzie. Jean always insisted that there was an understanding between Tom Kinsella and Lizzie, but I hardly think a man as keen as Tom could ever have been taken in by the likes of Lizzie," and the marchioness got up preparatory to making her departure.

"Why, Mother, to think of Cousin Sally's knowing Mr. Kinsella, too! You liked him, didn't you, Cousin Sally?" asked Molly eagerly. "He was on our steamer and so kind to us."

"Yes, my dear, I liked him very much and should like to see him again, and so would my Jean. I fancy a great many persons are kind to my little cousin," and she pinched Molly's blushing cheek. "Now, Milly, don't worry for one moment about an apartment as I am almost sure I know of a place that will just suit you. It is a studio apartment on the Rue Brea, just across the Luxembourg Garden from here. It belongs to an American artist named Bent. He and his wife are going to Italy for the winter and would be delighted to rent it furnished, I am sure. It is very superior to many of the studios in the Latin Quarter as it has a bathroom. But I am not going to tell you any more about it until I find out if you can get it, what the price is, and just what sleeping accommodations it has. I have my limousine at the door and shall go immediately to the Rue Brea, and to-night when you come to us for dinner I can tell you more. *Au revoir*, then, my long lost cousin," and she kissed Mrs. Brown on both cheeks.

"That is the first Frenchy thing she has done yet," thought Molly; and then when the elevator had slowly descended out of hearing distance she remarked to her mother: "How could anyone live in a foreign country for almost thirty years and stay so exactly like 'home folks'? Cousin Sally's accent is much more southern than yours and mine. Did you notice her 'sure' was almost 'sho' and she spoke of Lizzie Peck's dra-a-win' young men? I love her for keeping the same. And oh what fun to be going there to dinner! I can hardly wait for Judy to come home from the studio to tell her."

Mrs. Brown was equally pleased with her cousin's having remained so unaffected and looked forward with much pleasure to renewing the girlhood intimacy, and also to meeting the Marquis d'Ochtè, of whom his wife spoke so enthusiastically as "my Jean," and the son Philippe. She had some misgivings about the son because the literature of the day does not paint a young Frenchman in particularly desirable colors as the companion of girls; but she hoped that the mother's innate good sense had served to bring up the boy in the proper way. Then Molly and Judy could meet him as they would any young man from their own country, and he would understand their easy freedom of manner and of speech, different, she well knew, from that of the unmarried French girl. She determined to say nothing to the girls of the difference, as she did not want them changed or embarrassed by self-consciousness, and she felt sure of their having breeding and *savoir faire* to carry them through any situation with flying colors.

As the marchioness had indicated, she had married before Jean had succeeded to the estates and indeed before he had any idea of being the heir presumptive. His uncle, the Marquis d'Ochtè, was at the time a comparatively young man, a widower with a son of twelve;

and everyone expected that he would marry again and perhaps have other sons. Jean d'Ochtè, when she met him, was a rising young journalist, making, however, but a meager salary. His father was dead. His mother, Madame d'Ochtè, was a very superior woman and recognized Sally Bolling's worth in spite of the fact that she had but a tiny dot to bestow at her marriage. She saw her son's infatuation for the American girl and gave her consent to the marriage, without which, as is the law in France, they could not have been wed. Sally's alliance gave her the *entrée* into the most exclusive homes of the Faubourg St. Germain but she was not a whit impressed by it. She took her honors so simply and naturally that she won the hearts of all her husband's connection and they ended by applauding the leniency of Madame d'Ochtè in permitting the match, which they had formerly condemned as sentimental.

Jean and his wife spent their first married years living in the simplest style and Sally learned the economy for which the French are famous. Then came the windfall of fifty thousand dollars from Aunt Sarah Carmichael, which reconciled the exclusive Faubourg more than ever to the match; and then the death of the little cousin of Jean's, making him his uncle's heir; and finally the death of the uncle, which gave Jean the title of Marquis d'Ochtè. It meant giving up his profession, to which he was much attached; but the estates had to be looked after and the dignity of the title maintained; and now there was leisure for the reading and writing of plays, which had been his secret ambition.

Sally made a delightful marchioness. She had been accustomed to the best society in Kentucky and she declared good society was the same all over the world; as far as she could see the only way to get on was just to be yourself and not put on airs. She was very popular in the select circle to which the title of Marquise d'Ochtè admitted her but she did not confine herself to that circle; she knew all kinds and conditions of people, and never forgot a friend, no matter how humble.

Judy was very much excited at the prospect of dining with a live member of the old nobility, but her excitement was nothing to that of Mrs. Pace. That lady, when she received the message from Mrs.

Brown telling her they would not be at home for dinner as they would dine out, immediately climbed to the seventh story to find out where they were to dine, and on being informed of their destination, she went off into transports of delight. Her ardor was somewhat dampened when it was divulged that Judy was to be one of the party.

"Sally is very good natured but entirely too democratic for her position as the wife of one of the very oldest of the nobility in France. Of course she asked Miss Kean because of her friendship with your daughter," panted the irate dame, out of breath from her climb up two flights.

"I don't believe that was the only reason," said Molly, rather glad to give Mrs. Pace a dig after her report of her darling Judy. "Cousin Sally said she had been anxious to meet Miss Kean from what you had told her of my friend; so you are really responsible for the pleasure in store for her."

"Well, I only hope she appreciates the honor done her," spluttered Mrs. Pace. "What are you going to wear? A dinner in the Faubourg and the Opera afterward calls for the very best in your wardrobe."

"Perhaps you had better advise us about our clothes," said Mrs. Brown sweetly, remembering what her cousin had said of Mrs. Pace's kind heart and how she humored her by seeming to let her boss her. "I have a very pretty black crêpe de Chine. I think I am too old to go décolleté, but I am sure this is suitable, especially as I have nothing else."

"It is perfectly suitable, and if you take my advice you will wear it and leave the neck exactly as it is with that lovely old lace finishing it off in a V. For pity sakes, don't tell Sally you are too old for low necks as she is about your age and wears décolleté gowns on every occasion where one is warranted," said Mrs. Pace, much pleased at being taken into anyone's confidence on the subject of clothes or anything else.

Molly, taking her cue from her mother, then got out her dress and showed it to the eager landlady.

"It is lovely and just your color. Sally used to be given to that blue when she was young, but she says now she is too big and red to wear anything but brown or black. You must have a taxi to go in. I will attend to it for you. I hope Miss Kean will not do herself up in any fantastic, would-be artistic get-up, but will do you and your daughter credit, to say nothing of me, after I have got her this invitation," and Mrs. Pace bustled off, filled with importance.

Mrs. Brown and the girls, left alone at last, dressed themselves with the greatest care for the occasion, realizing what it meant to dine with the nobility and then go to the far-famed Opera.

"Only think, the tomb of Napoleon, dinner with a marquis and the Opera, all in one day! I almost wish we had put off the tomb until to-morrow. Our impressions are coming too fast," exclaimed Molly.

CHAPTER VII.

THE FAUBOURG.

At the toot of the horn, the porte cochère of the Hotel d'Ochtè was thrown open by a venerable porter and the taxi containing Mrs. Brown and the girls swept into the court in great style. How beautiful it was! The soft color of the stone walls blended with the formal box bushes and tubs of oleanders; here and there a wrought-iron lantern projected from the pilasters; rows of snub-nosed caryatides held up little balconies, also of wrought iron, of the most delicate design and workmanship. Judy held her breath at the effect of line and color and wondered if she would ever know the inmates well enough to be allowed to make a picture of the court.

They were met in the hall by the most gracious and least formal of hostesses and taken immediately to her boudoir to remove their wraps.

"And this is Miss Julia Kean, the friend of my cousin, as the easy lessons in French put it. I am afraid I shall just have to call you Judy, my dear, and not start out trying to 'miss' you. And Molly in my own blue! Ah, child, for the first time in my life I tremble for the affections of my Jean! There is something about the combination of that particular blue with red hair that goes to his head. Milly, you are beautiful! How proud I am of my kin!" And the marchioness chattered on, leading them down a long, dim hall, hung with tapestries and armor, to the library.

"We live in our library. It is so much cosier than the great salon and we feel more at home in the smaller room; and here we can talk without having to shout across space."

The door was opened at their approach by Philippe who bowed low as they entered and stood aside, while they were introduced to his father, the Marquis d'Ochtè.

The marquis was a very interesting-looking man, tall for a Frenchman, with merry brown eyes and a black, closely cut, pointed beard. His hair was iron gray, thick and rather bushy. His manner was very cordial and all of the ladies were secretly relieved to find that he spoke English fluently, if with an accent.

Philippe was a handsomer man than his father, having that rare combination of coloring: dark eyes and golden hair. He wore a pointed beard, too, as is the almost invariable custom of Frenchmen; his eye was as merry as his father's and he had inherited his mother's strong chin, big honest mouth and perfect teeth. The d'Ochtè family certainly made a wonderfully fine looking trio. The marchioness was radiant in black velvet and diamonds, her neck and arms beautiful and white, her abundant hair parted in the middle and done in a loose knot on her neck. She was a very distinguished looking woman and worthy to take her place with royalty as well as with the nobility. Years had touched her but lightly; but the eternal youth in her heart, as in that of Mrs. Brown, was what gave her the charm of expression and manner.

Cordial relations were established immediately between old and young.

"There is nothing like a good American handshake to make strangers acquainted," said the host, looking admiringly at his wife's cousins and their attractive companion, Judy, who in spite of Mrs. Pace's fears that she might get herself up in "paint rags," was most artistically gowned in old-rose messaline. "It is more pleasure than I can express to meet the cousins of my Sara; also Mademoiselle Kean, of whom we have heard much from the respected Madame Pace," he added with a mischievous twinkle.

"Heavens, how must I behave if Mrs. Pace has already given me a character?" exclaimed Judy. "Must I be as she says I am, or must I be as she wants me to be?"

"Be yourself, and you will be as we want you," said the marchioness, kindly. "Jean and Philippe do not have the chance to meet many American girls and they do not, as a rule, care to meet Henny's boarders, who are usually dry-as-dust old maids, especially the ones Henny recommends."

"Oh, please don't change yourselves, any of you," begged Philippe in a voice and accent so southern that it was amusing coming from a veritable Frenchman. "All my life, I have longed to meet some of my cousins and to hear more of the Kentucky stories, and of Chatsworth and the Carmichael place. Does Cousin Sarah Carmichael, Mrs. Clay, I believe she is now, still take the biggest piece of cake, and are the beech trees as beautiful as they were when my mother used to play under them with you, Cousin Mildred?"

"Oh, Philippe, you should not tell tales out of school! Sarah is Milly's sister and she might not like the cake reminiscences. Sarah was mighty grabby, though, wasn't she, Milly? I am afraid she will never forgive me for getting the legacy from Aunt Sarah Carmichael. You see we were both named for her and Sarah naturally expected an equal division if not the 'biggest piece of cake,' and when the whole fifty thousand came to me, it was a sad blow to Sarah. But she was quite comfortable and Jean and I were the needy members of the family, as far as money went. That was all we did need as we had everything else," and the marchioness laid her hand lightly on her husband's bushy hair whence he gently drew it down to his cheek.

Mrs. Brown could not help smiling over Sister Clay and the big piece of cake. She remembered how the two Sarahs had always been at daggers drawn. Her sister was much older than Sally Bolling and had always been critical of the lively girl who had repaid her by laughing at her and cracking jokes at her expense.

"Yes indeed, Philippe, the beeches are even more beautiful having had some years since then to grow. Trees are one of the things that improve with age. I hope you will come to Kentucky and make us a long visit and see all of your kin and their homes," said Mrs. Brown cordially.

"That would be fine, if the mother and father could come, too. You don't know how beautiful your southern tongue sounds to me, Cousin Mildred. You say 'kin' just as my mother does and as I do. I am laughed at by my English friends for my way of speaking their language, but I would not give up my southern accent for worlds."

Dinner was announced, interrupting Philippe, and they made their way to the *salle a manger*. The marquis gave his arm to Mrs. Brown; Judy fell to the share of the handsome young son; and the marchioness put her arm affectionately around Molly's waist.

"My dear," she said, "having you with us is a pleasure, indeed. I wish I had a daughter just like you. I think your mother might spare you to me. She has two other daughters and four sons. That is too much for any woman."

"You had better not say that to mother," laughed Molly. "The only time I ever saw her lose her temper with Aunt Clay, who would try the patience of a saint, was when Aunt Clay intimated that it would be much more economical if there had been only half of us, three children and a half instead of seven. I was a tiny little girl, but I can remember how I crawled under the table I was so scared. I had never seen mother get really mad before and she turned on Aunt Clay in such a rage that I felt sorry for her. You know it must have been pretty bad if I felt sorry for Aunt Clay, for she is the one person in the world I can't like."

"Molly, we are alike in more ways than one! She is an abomination unto me! Sarah Clay made my childhood unhappy. You see, I had no regular home as my mother and I were very poor. We spent much of our time visiting and Cousin George Carmichael, your grandfather, was goodness itself to us. The Carmichael place was more like home than any other to me. I simply loved it and spent many happy hours playing with your dear mother; but Sarah never lost a chance to rub it in on me that I was in a measure a dependent. As a child it would cut me to the quick; but as I got older and made my visits at Cousin George's, I would retaliate by making game of my older cousin; and no one can abide being made fun of. I tell you I gave her tit for tat and usually came out ahead. But we must stop this whispering. Your mother can't stand any criticism of her sister. Some day we can get together and say all the mean things we've a mind to about old Sarah!" Then the marchioness was transformed in the twinkling of an eye from the naughty Sally Boiling to the gracious hostess, seeing that her guests were seated and leading the conversation into the most agreeable channels.

The dinner was perfect, every detail in absolute taste, served beautifully but with an elegant simplicity. Molly made mental notes on the sauce with the fish, trying to find out without asking what was in it; and then the gravy with the filet of beef occupied her attention. Such a wonderful gravy with a character all its own. She remembered what Edwin Green had told her of the Frenchman who was visiting America. When asked his impressions of the country, he had said: "America is a country with a thousand different religions and one sauce." She wondered what Miss Morse would think of this gravy, and smiled as she recalled the lecture on gravies delivered by that highly educated teacher of domestic science and the smooth, perfect specimen she demonstrated, with no more flavor than Miss Morse herself.

"What is the little joke my Cousin Mollee is having all to herself," asked the marquis.

Molly frankly confessed what had made her smile, since her cousin wanted to know, and of course in her confession praise of the gravy had to be included.

"Brava, brava," and the Marquis d'Ochtè clapped his hands. "She is like my Sara in all ways. She is also a discriminator in foods. This gravy, my dear Mademoiselle, is the *chef d'[oe]uvre* of my chef. You notice the butler, Jules, has left the room. *Pourquoi* does he go? He cannot wait to tell Gaston, the chef, that Madame's cousin from across the seas has been so gracious as to praise his work of art. If you will turn ever so little you will see the happy face of Gaston peeping in to view the beautiful young lady."

Molly turned, and sure enough, tip-toeing to see over the shoulder of Jules the butler, was Gaston, his face radiant.

"Molly is a wonderful cook herself," said Judy. "She has an instinct for food that is truly remarkable. At college an invitation to a Molly Brown spread was looked upon with greater reverence than being asked to have tea with the President. But has she not learned from Aunt Mary, that dear old colored woman who cooks like an angel? We trembled for fear that the domestic science teacher would ruin Molly's touch and make her too academic, but I hope it hasn't."

"Dear Aunt Mary, I had almost forgotten her!" exclaimed the marchioness. "Don't tell me you can make Aunt Mary's spoon corn bread, Molly! If you can, I'll make the Bents move out of their studio to-morrow so you can move in. And I'll come to live with you and get you to make me some for every meal until all the cornmeal to be purchased at the American grocers' is used up!"

"Indeed she can, Sally, and many things besides. Aunt Mary has initiated her into all the secrets of her trade," said Mrs. Brown. "I remember so well hearing the old woman say to Molly, when she was a little girl, 'Ef you wan' ter know how ter make bread, you have ter begin at de beginnin'. Now yeast is de fust an' maindest thing and tater yeast is the onliest kin' fit ter use, an' you can't git taters 'thout diggin' 'em; so fer the fust step, s'pose you go an' dig some taters.' So, you see, my Molly can do it all."

"Oh, how I love to hear about Aunt Mary!" sighed Philippe. "Am I to have some of this ambrosial bread, too, Cousin Molly?"

"Yes, indeed, but I am afraid the meal we get in Paris will not be right. Tell us, Cousin Sally, about the studio in the Rue Brea. Can we get it? We have had so many things to talk about, we have not asked you about it."

"The Bents expect to go to Italy for six months and are very much pleased to have good tenants in their absence. I am going to take you and your mother and Miss Kean, if she can come, to see the place to-morrow morning. The rent is reasonable, ridiculously cheap even, one hundred and twenty-five francs a month."

Mrs. Brown's face fell at the rental named by her cousin. The marchioness saw it and gave a merry laugh. "I know just what you are doing, Milly; you are thinking in dollars. I said a hundred and twenty-five *francs*; that is only twenty-five dollars."

"Oh, how silly I am! I did think you meant dollars. Of course, that is cheap and well within our means. We are so grateful to you, Sally, and I am sure it will suit," said Mrs. Brown, blushing at her mistake, which she need not have done as it is no easy matter to think in foreign money.

The dinner went gaily on. Molly and Judy told Philippe all about Wellington College, and he in turn had much to tell them of Nancy, where he had been studying forestry after his course at the Sorbonne. The marquis and marchioness had many questions to ask Mrs. Brown of the relatives in Kentucky. The talk was interesting and delightful and they felt as though they had known one another always.

They lingered over their coffee and cheese until the butler announced that the limousine was at the door ready to take them to the Opera. There was a general move for wraps and gloves, but Philippe stopped his mother long enough to embrace her and whisper in her ear: "Both of them are jewels and I can't tell which one is the more precious"; and Molly and Judy, unconscious of their being rivals, hugged each other in Cousin Sally's boudoir and said in chorus: "What an Adonis!"

CHAPTER VIII.

THE OPERA.

The ride through the brilliantly lighted streets; across the Seine with its myriad of small boats with their red and green lanterns; through the Place du Carrousel where the Louvre loomed up dark and mysterious; under the arch and across the Rue de Rivoli; then into the Avenue de l'Opera, seemed to Mrs. Brown and Molly the very most delightful experience of their "great adventure." It was an old story to Judy but one she could not hear too often, this Paris at night; and the marchioness confessed that after thirty years, the Avenue, if you approached it as they were doing, gave her a thrill that was ever new and wonderful. They proceeded slowly, as the procession of automobiles was endless.

"The horse is almost an extinct animal in Paris," said the marquis to Mrs. Brown, who had remarked that she feared she was coming to Paris too late to see the much written of type of "cab, cab horse and cabby." One sees occasionally a specimen of the old days: rickety cab, thin horse and fat, red-faced *cocher*; but such an equipage seems to be in demand only by the very timid who are afraid to trust themselves to the modern means of locomotion. Those poor souls are not, as a rule, on the boulevards at this hour, but shut snugly behind doors, locked and barred, safe from the "dread Apaches and all the terrors of the night."

"I love automobiles," exclaimed Molly, "but nothing could ever take the place of a horse to me, even a poor, abused, old cab horse "

"Ah then, you can ride!" cried the delighted Philippe. "And you, too, Miss Kean? American girls are the finest on earth surely," (only he said "sholy"). "We have horses at *Roche Craie* and all of us ride. Mother is a splendid horsewoman."

"Yes indeed, I am going to ride just as long as a horse can be found big enough to carry me," laughed the marchioness. "Sometimes I think my poor beast must look like a pet duck I had when I was a child. It got run over by a wagon, and my old mammy said, 'Yo' lil duck got run over, honey chile. He is right down in the back but still able to bear up!'

"But it is fine that you girls can ride, and when you come to visit us at *Roche Craie* you can have some famous gallops. I hate the English riding horse with his eternal trotting and the rider working himself to death posting. Our horses are good Kentucky riding stock with gaits. I hope you brought your riding habits."

"I did!" and "I did!" said Molly and Judy almost in the same breath.

"I never move without my riding habit, bathing suit and skates," declared Judy. "I learned my lesson about my bathing suit once when I spent the summer in camp with Papa. I did not know we would have any bathing worthy the name and did not put mine in the trunk. When we got there we found that the only form of bath that could be had was in a creek as there was not even a basin in camp, and there was I without a bathing suit! Papa was furious at my stupidity. We were miles from any kind of shop. 'Necessity is the mother of invention,' so I took a big laundry bag, cut slits for arms and legs, tied the draw string around my neck, and with a neat belt I looked quite chic. It did not give me much freedom for swimming but I could at least get the necessary bath."

Every one roared at the picture Judy drew of herself tied up in the laundry bag and just then they got out of the jam on the Avenue, crossed the great Boulevard des Italiens, and stopped at the beautiful entrance to the Opera.

The d'Ochtè box was in the first tier and proved very roomy and comfortable, commanding an excellent view of the house as well as the stage.

"We have come early on purpose," said the marchioness, "as I wanted you to see the house fill. I can point out any celebrities I happen to know before the performance begins."

The girls and Mrs. Brown were seated in the front, with the host and hostess and their son in the back of the box. There were two extra seats, but madame declared that she liked to have some left for visitors.

"*Louise* is the opera of all others to introduce strangers to Paris," explained Philippe to Molly. "It is Paris, Paris sounds, Paris sights, the tragedy and comedy of Paris."

Molly was devoutly thankful that she had bought the libretto of the opera of *Louise* when she and her mother had ventured out to see the tomb of Napoleon after the visit of Cousin Sally in the morning; and when they were taking their much needed rest before dressing for dinner in the Faubourg, she had read it aloud to her mother.

"I was so afraid I might miss something," she explained ingenuously to her cousin. "You see, mother and I want to see and hear everything we can. We have done so little traveling and seen so little in our lives that this coming to Paris is like a visit to fairyland to us. I am afraid I'll wake up and find it is all a dream."

"I feel as though I were in a dream, too," said Philippe. "I have had so little chance to talk to girls like you and Miss Kean. *La jeune fille, bien élevèe,* in France is so missish and afraid to speak out to a man. You and your friend look me straight in the eye without the least affectation of timidity, just as though you were boys instead of girls; and at the same time you are delightfully feminine. It is a strange thing to me to watch one of these girls of my country, with downcast eyes and so much modesty she can hardly speak above a whisper. The moment she becomes *madame* all this timidity disappears, and in the twinkling of an eye she is the charming young married woman, full of all the arts and graces. The transformation is so sudden, it makes one doubt the sincerity of the former modesty. Mother says the French girl is thus because it is what the average Frenchman wants, the old story of supply and demand. But I am half Anglo-Saxon and want no such person for my wife. My mother has spoiled me, and I can never be happy with a hypocrite."

Molly smiled, thinking that while her cousin was declaring himself Anglo-Saxon, he was certainly not talking like one. Such candor is seldom seen in the male Anglo-Saxon. His warmth and fervor were decidedly French.

The house was beginning to fill and many glasses were leveled at the box of Madame la Marquise d'Ochtè. The general verdict was that it was a very effective grouping. Certainly there were not two middle-aged women in the whole audience more distinguished looking or handsomer than the marchioness and her cousin; nor were there two fresher or sweeter looking girls, charming in their eagerness to see and not for one moment conscious that they were attracting any attention. The marquis and Philippe formed a pleasing background of masculinity to these beautiful women.

The opening scene, *Louise's* garret room in her father's house with the view through the window of her lover's studio; the duet with her lover in which she tells him of her father's refusal to their marriage; and then her promise to run away with him in event of her parent's persisting in his hard-hearted resolution to separate them, seemed to Molly most wonderful and touching; but when the mother came in and berated the lover, *Julien*, as "a rascal, a starveling, a dissipator"; and when *Louise* defended him as being "so good, so courageous," and the mother retaliated by calling him the pillar of a wine shop and attempted to beat her daughter, Molly covered her eyes and wept, all unconscious of the amused glances of the occupants of the neighboring box.

But in a moment she was watching again: The father has come in and there is some sort of reconciliation between him and Louise, although her mother is still furious and slaps her in the face when she takes up for him; then the father interferes and embraces *Louise*, and they are finally all seated around the table, the mother with her sewing, the father with his pipe, when *Louise* starts to read aloud from the newspaper: "The Spring Season is most brilliant. All Paris is in holiday garb." *Louise* stops reading and after a moment sobs: "Paris— —" and the curtain slowly descends.

There was a storm of applause, and Molly came to the realization that she was in a fair way to have a red nose if she did not control her emotions. She gave a sad little smile and hoped that Philippe would talk to Judy and let her be sure of herself before she trusted her voice.

As she looked out over the "sea of upturned faces," she saw Mr. Kinsella and Pierce in the pit. They were applauding vigorously but Mr. Kinsella had an eye on their box, evidently in hopes of recognition. Molly gave him a delighted bow and then told her mother and the marchioness of his presence. The marquis overheard her remark.

"What! Do you mean my old friend, Tom Kinsella? Where, where? Point him out to me. I'll go and bring him to our box."

He hurried out and made his way to where the Kinsellas were seated. The twenty-five years since he had seen his American friend were forgotten. He remembered him as the glowing, enthusiastic boy, for whom the whole Latin Quarter felt such sympathy when he had to give up his beloved art and go into business. It escaped his mind entirely that time had not stood still with Tom Kinsella any more than with him. Jean d'Ochtè made a very natural mistake. He put his arm lovingly around Pierce and in his impulsive French way said: "*Mon cher Tom, je t'embrasse.*"

Pierce looked up, very much amused at being hugged at the Opera by a distinguished looking French gentleman with a black beard and bushy, gray hair. Mr. Kinsella rose from his seat and clasping the marquis by the hand, exclaimed:

"Jean, how splendid to meet you on this my first night in Paris after all these years! Don't apologize for mistaking my nephew for me," and he introduced Pierce to him, calling him "Monsieur d'Ochtè," being entirely ignorant of the fact of his old friend's having inherited a title and estates. "Now tell me of Madame. I do hope I am to be allowed to see her."

"*Certainment,* my friend. She now awaits you in the box where we are entertaining Sara's cousins, Mrs. and Miss Brown, of Kentukee, also a charming *jeune fille,* by name Miss Kean."

Uncle and nephew were led, willing captives, to fill the unoccupied seats in the box. Mrs. Brown and Molly were delighted to see them again, and Judy and Pierce plunged into a discussion of art schools and pictures. The marchioness was overjoyed to meet a friend from the old Bohemian days and her husband was like a boy in his enthusiasm over this long lost companion. Philippe looked a little sad and downcast, although he was studiously polite to the strangers. He had been having such a splendid time with the girls that he could not help resenting the interruption to his pleasure caused by the entrance of these two Americans. He was secretly glad when the curtain went up and the whole party was forced to give their attention to the stage.

The next act, in front of the wine shop, the lover *Julien* and his companions playing and making horseplay, had the note of true comedy and Molly could find nothing to weep over, for which she was truly thankful. She whispered to Mr. Kinsella that when there was anything to cry over, she simply had to cry, and he said:

"I see you have what Mr. Dooley calls 'the stage delusion'. It is a delightful quality to feel the reality of the drama and not remember there is any 'behind the scenes'. I fancy at this minute *Louise*, who got a little husky in that duet with *Julien*, when she promised to leave her mother and father and come to him, is off in her dressing room spraying her throat and gargling with peroxide to get her voice in trim for the third act. In that she has a long and very beautiful love scene in the little home at the apex of the Butte Montmartre where *Julien* takes her."

"Why did you come to Paris so soon?" asked Mrs. Brown just then. "You meant to exhaust the sights of Antwerp before leaving, did you not?"

"Well, you see the sights exhausted me before I exhausted them, and then, like *Louise*, I felt the call of Paris. We got in only an hour ago, and after a very hasty dinner came to the Opera. *Louise* seemed to me to be the very best introduction I could give my nephew to this wonderful city."

"That is exactly what I have been saying to my cousin Molly!" broke in Philippe. "It seems to me that Charpentier has given the true Paris with all of its charm and its dangers. Of course one should see this opera for the first time in the spring of the year, as that is when Paris is most alluring and in that season the scene is laid."

"Molly, look in the second tier of boxes almost directly opposite us and see if that good looking young woman in the rather *outré* gown is an acquaintance of yours," said the marchioness. "She has been looking at our box steadily ever since we arrived."

"Her face is familiar but I can't place her. Judy, see if you know her," said Molly, as she adjusted Mr. Kinsella's opera glasses to her eyes. She and Judy got the focus at the same moment and exclaimed in unison: "Frances Andrews!"

"She is a girl we knew in our freshman year at college" explained Molly to her Cousin Sally. "I remember she came to Paris to join her grandmother, but we have never seen or heard of her since she left college. She was a very peculiar person but clever and bright, and always awfully nice to me."

"Humph!" sniffed Judy. "I'd like to see the person who isn't nice to you, you old saint! The only thing I ever liked about Frances Andrews was that she got into bigger scrapes than I did and made my misdemeanors seem small in comparison. She was clever enough, I'll grant you that, but peculiar is a kind adjective to use in describing that girl. Why, Molly, she was the most unpopular girl at Wellington. Even her own class did not stand by her. She was crooked, as crooked as a snake."

"Oh, Judy, there was a lot of good in Frances, but she got in bad with her class and could not redeem herself somehow. She was so young, too, and I haven't a doubt that she is vastly improved," and Molly caught the eager eye of the handsome girl in the opposite box and gave her a cordial bow.

In a moment an usher brought a card to the door of the d'Ochtè box. On it was scrawled the following note:

"Molly darling: I am wild to see you. Give me your address and I'll come to-morrow. — Frances."

Molly wrote the address of the *Maison Pace* and said she would be glad to see her, but had an engagement for the time named. She was a little sorry that Frances had turned up, as she knew that Judy would refuse to see any good in her and did not know just how the very sophisticated young woman would impress her mother. But Molly was not one to turn her back on any one who was fond of her and she had always been sorry for Frances, feeling in the old days at college that she had been too easily condemned by her classmates. "There was good in her," reiterated Molly to herself, "and there still is, and I am going to be nice to her. Judy can be as stand-offish as she pleases. I know mother will be kind; she always is."

The last act of *Louise* was the most wonderful of all and Molly felt herself becoming so filled with emotion that she feared she would spill over again. She was grateful to Mr. Kinsella when he said to her in an undertone: "The gargle evidently did her good as the huskiness has gone." She smiled in spite of herself and the tears had to go.

It was over all too soon. *Louise's* father, after he realizes that *Louise* has gone for good to her devoted lover in Montmartre, gazes through the garret window at Paris, which, lighted, seems like a thousand-eyed monster to the old man. He shakes his fist in a rage and cries, "Oh, *Paris!*"

As they put on their wraps, Molly heard the marchioness whisper to her husband: "Ah, Jean, your mother was wise to let us marry, wise and good. How much better it would have been for this poor old man if he could have let youth have its say!"

"Ah, my Sara, indeed she was. And now *ma mère* can still hear the voice of Paris calling as did *Louise* in the first act, and she does not have to curse it as did *la père* in the last." And the marquis disguised a fervent hug in the pretext of helping his wife with her cloak.

CHAPTER IX.

THE POSTSCRIPT.

The Bents' studio apartment proved to be exactly the thing for Mrs. Brown and the girls, and arrangements were made with the artist and his wife to have it turned over to them in ten days, which would just fill out their time at *Maison Pace*.

The apartment consisted of a large studio, kitchenette and two small bedrooms. The plan was for Mrs. Brown to have one of the bedrooms and Elise O'Brien the other, while Molly and Judy, to their unbounded delight, were to sleep in a balcony that ran across one end of the studio. The Marquise d'Ochtè explained to them that this was quite customary in Bohemia, and that she and her husband had occupied a similar roost for several years during their early married life.

"I am versed in many a makeshift and this minute could come to live in the Latin Quarter on half of what you, with your extravagant American notions, will spend," declared the marchioness, as she showed our friends over the apartment. "Now this is my advice for the conducting of your *ménage*, Milly, but I am not like Henny Pace to get riled if you do not take it. Get your own breakfast, which is a simple matter in France, having fresh rolls and butter sent in every morning and making your own coffee or chocolate; take your *déjeuner à la fourchette*, I mean your luncheon at a restaurant; and then leave your dinners to circumstances, sometimes having them at home or going out as the occasion offers.

"Get a servant to come in and clean for you every morning by the hour, but do not have a regular *bonne*. It would be a useless expense and then there is no sense in your having to slave over housekeeping. The way for foreigners to become acquainted with Paris is to see the restaurants, and there are so many you need not get tired of the cooking in any one. All I ask of you is to have a regular Kentucky supper for me some night with— —but never mind what with, it will be sure to be what I want if Molly cooks it."

71

Molly was busy inspecting the kitchenette, which Mrs. Bent was showing with much pride as it was quite unique in the Latin Quarter. There was a tiny gas range, a convenience not often enjoyed as gas was a luxury not as a rule afforded in Bohemia. The floor was of octagonal, terra cotta tiles and there was a high mullioned window over the infinitesimal sink. Long-handled copper skillets and stew pans were ranged along the walls, suspended from hooks; and a strangely colored china press filled with an odd assortment of dishes was at one side.

Mrs. Bent laughed when she saw Molly examining the press. "That is inherited from Mr. Bent's student days. It is a plain deal closet, colored with palette scrapings. It is always a great stunt with students to make something like this. Mr. Bent has long ago outgrown it as a studio furnishing and will have nothing short of mahogany around him, but it is too roomy and useful for me to give up, so it is banished to the limbo of the kitchen. I have known students to clean their palettes many times a day just to get a little more scrapings on their presses."

The effect was a peculiarly deep, rich tone and Judy declared that she liked it.

"It looks like the shadows in some of Monet's landscapes, dark, but clear, with light all through them. Some day I am going to make a press just like this one if I have to clean my palette a hundred times a day to get scrapings."

The apartment was on the ground floor and one entered across a very pretty paved court which had green tubs of evergreens here and there along the wall. The indoor studio balcony, where Judy and Molly were to sleep, had a long casement that opened on a tiny iron balcony which overhung the court. There were four similar balconies belonging to the neighboring studios and all had porch boxes filled with ivy or chrysanthemums, making a wonderful effect of color.

Judy was Judy-like, entranced. She stepped upon the balcony and holding out her arms to the tubbed spruce trees, exclaimed in a melodramatic voice:

"'O Romeo, Romeo, wherefore art thou Romeo?
Deny thy father and refuse thy name:
Or, if thou wilt not, be but sworn my love,
And I'll no longer be a Capulet.'"

Suddenly what should she see, from the open door of the opposite studio, but the faun-like face of Pierce Kinsella, grinning delightedly at the unexpected encounter. He proved himself equal to the occasion and said in a low and feeling voice:

"'Shall I hear more, or shall I speak at this?'"

And Judy came back with:

"'How cam'st thou hither, tell me, and wherefore?
The orchard walls are high and hard to climb,
And the place death, considering who thou art,
If any of my kinsmen find thee here.'"

And Pierce answered:

"'With love's light wings did I o'erperch these walls;
For stony limits cannot hold love out,
And what love can do that dares love attempt;
Therefore thy kinsmen are no let to me.'"

By this time Mr. Kinsella had come out into the court and Molly, hearing the spouting of so much poetry, joined Judy on the balcony to see what was going on. She and Mr. Kinsella applauded loudly until the windows of the two other balconies opened, and from one the head of a long-haired man and from the other that of a short-haired woman were poked out.

"Poetry aside, Mr. Kinsella, what are you and Pierce doing here in the Rue Brea?" called Judy.

"We are looking at a studio that is for rent. And what are you doing here, please?"

"Sitting under our own vine and fig tree, sir! At least, it will be ours in about ten days," answered Molly.

"You don't mean it! Well, if this isn't luck! Pierce, I'll go back and sign up with the concierge immediately. Such neighbors as these would make the meanest studio desirable and, after all, these are pretty good rooms. We could hardly do better in the Quarter."

Pierce was pleased to have the matter settled, as he felt himself to be among friends and had visions of many good times in store for him after working hours with the three bright girls and Mrs. Brown, who was even more attractive to him than the girls. Mr. Kinsella had assured Mrs. Brown that Elise would be sure to fall in with any plans that good lady may have made for her, and he answered for Mrs. Huntington's acquiescence in any arrangements he saw fit to bring about for her daughter. She had really washed her hands of the matter, and had given him to understand that since he had interfered and insisted upon Elise's having a chance to go on with her much interrupted art studies, he could go ahead and place her where he chose. For her part, she declared, it made no difference one way or the other. She had seen too much of Bohemia in the old days to want ever to cross the borderland again. Mr. Kinsella felt sure she had secretly hoped that Mrs. Brown would want Elise with her, and he only awaited their arrival from Brussels to let them know of the studio apartment in the Rue Brea and of the cordial welcome Elise O'Brien would have from all three of the ladies concerned.

The next ten days were very busy and exciting ones. Judy and Pierce plunged into their drawing with renewed zest. Pierce was at Julien's, too, but as the men's school is in an entirely different part of Paris from the women's, he and Judy saw each other only in picture galleries or on the delightful jaunts that the whole crowd took. The *Maison Pace* was not a very pleasant place to make a call, as there was always a bunch of snuffy old maids huddled together in the parlor, knitting shawls and swapping tales of the good and bad pensions they had encountered in their travels. When a caller braved the ordeal, they always stopped knitting and talking and sat spellbound, intent on not losing one word of the visitor's conversation.

Mr. Kinsella and Pierce made one essay, but the occasion was so stiff and formal and Mrs. Pace so monopolizing that they determined never to repeat it, but to wait until their friends were installed in their own apartment. That longed-for time arrived quickly enough for Molly and her mother, who were sight-seeing in a most systematic manner, with Baedecker in one hand and Hare's "Walks in Paris" in the other. They would come home tired and footsore but very happy and enthusiastic.

Molly wrote Professor Green that she felt like the little girl at the fair, who, when her mother noticed she lagged behind and asked her if she were tired, said: "My hands and feet are tired, but my face isn't."

"We do become weary unto death but each morning we get up with renewed zest," she wrote, "with so many wonderful things to see before nightfall. One thing that bothers us is having to dress and sit through a formal dinner with the eagle eye of Mrs. Pace upon us. We are looking forward to the time when we shall be in our own apartment, where we need not dress for dinner unless we have a mind to. My Cousin Philippe d'Ochtè declares that already my mother and I know more about Paris than he does. We are trying to be systematic in our sight-seeing and not to hurry, as we have the winter before us, but at every corner and square there is something interesting to find out about.

"Philippe is very kind to us and ready to escort us through any parts of the city where he thinks it best for women not to go alone. For my part, I think we could go anywhere we wished. The Parisians are so obliging and courteous, and so far no one has been the least rude to us. The old maids in our pension have many tales to tell of the encounters they have had with impertinent men, and one lady declares that she never goes on the street without being insulted. But I agree with Mr. Kean who says: 'If you have some business to attend to—and attend to it, you women can go anywhere in the world you want to in perfect safety.'

"I have not begun my studies yet, as my time has been so taken up with seeing the places of interest, but Philippe is going to see that I am put in the proper class in French Lit. at the Sorbonne where he has obtained a very important degree. He says there are several English and American women there, so I shall not feel strange.

"I am so glad your orchard home is coming on so well. Kent writes us that it is already beginning to look like a house. The rough stone chimneys and foundations are lovely, I know, and will make such a beautiful support for English ivy.

"We are looking forward to Christmas with great eagerness. This is the first Christmas I have had with my mother for five years and the first one she has spent away from all of her other children ever. I shall have to make a noise like seven Browns to keep her from being homesick."

Here Molly stopped and reflected that some of those five Christmases she had spent in the company of Professor Edwin Green and she wondered if he would remember it, too; and if he would miss her as she felt she was missing him, in spite of all the delightful things she was doing and seeing. "I know he is not thinking of me at all and I am a goose to waste any sentiment on him. I have never had a single letter from him I could not show mother and Judy. When Judy gets a letter from Kent she never shows it to us, but takes it to her own room and evidently gets great satisfaction from its perusal, as she always comes out beaming. Ah me! I am sure I shall die an old maid,—but anyhow I do not intend to knit shawls and sit around a boarding house talking about the food!"

When poor Professor Green received the letter, part of which is given above, he, too, was plunged into sad reflections. He reached for a pretty azure paper weight that always stood on his desk and reminded him of a certain pair of blue, blue eyes, and looking into it as though he were crystal-gazing, he shook his head mournfully and said: "Ah, Molly, you little know how you hurt me! And still, what right have I to expect anything else from you? I see you now being conducted around Paris by your Cousin Philippe. I'll be bound he thinks you need a courier even when you go to a Duval restaurant, the sly dog. I know his type: small and dark, with a pointed beard and insinuating manner.

"Here I am tied to Wellington and these hated classes and lectures, when I hoped to be in Paris acting courier for Molly instead of this disgusting foreigner, who won't know how to appreciate her— —But what an ass I am! I don't know that Philippe is disgusting, and from what Miss Molly says of his mother, the marchioness, she must be charming.

"I do wish she would not write so coolly of my 'orchard home.' I should think she would know by telepathy that I always think of it as 'Molly Brown's Orchard Home.' I was a fool to take Mrs. Brown's advice and not tell Molly of my love. It may be too late now, and then what shall I do?"

The distinguished professor of English at Wellington College groaned aloud. His housekeeper, who was bringing in his tea, heard him and almost dropped the tray in her alarm.

"And is it the schtomic ache ye be ahfter havin'?"

"No, Mrs. Brady, it is higher up than the stomach. I am glad to see my tea. 'The beverage which cheers but does not inebriate' may make me feel better."

"Phwat ye need is a wife to look ahfter ye and keep ye straight. Schmokin', schmokin' all the time an' brroodin' over the fire is not good for a young gintleman. An' your disk and floor littered up wit' paaperrs and ashes."

The kindly old soul began to clear off the untidy desk and stooped to pick up a piece of paper that had fallen from Molly's letter without Professor Green's having read it or noticed its existence. She started to put it in the waste basket, but the professor noticed the action, being, like most scholars, impatient of having his books and papers touched. In fact, he had over his desk a framed rubbing of Shakespeare's epitaph which he had once confided to Molly he kept there especially to scare Mrs. Brady and make her let his things alone:

> "Good friend for Iesus sake forbeare
> To digg ye dust encloased heare
> Bleste be ye man yt spares the stones
> And curst be he yt moves my bones."

"Wait, my good Mrs. Brady! What is that you are throwing away?"

"Nawthin' but a bit o' blue paaperr, Profissorr. To be shure there's a schrap o' writin' on the back. Blue things always brring to me mind the swate eyes o' Miss Molly Brown, the saints protict her" and she handed the stray piece of thin, blue, foreign letter paper to the eager young man, who clutched it and smoothed it out and read the following postscript:

"My cousins, the d'Ochtès, have been very anxious to get up a party and take us to Fontainebleau to see the palace and then drive through the forest; but I have done everything to keep from going and I hope the scheme has fallen through. You have told me so much of the wonderful forest and the walk from Fontainebleau to Barbizon that I am hoping to see the place for the first time with you. The spring is the time to see it, anyhow, I am sure, and perhaps by then you can find a suitable substitute and have a holiday."

Professor Green looked up from the perusal of the little half sheet of paper with his face beaming. What can't a woman put in a postscript? The pain, which he had confessed to Mrs. Brady was a little higher up than his stomach, had entirely disappeared. He was no longer jealous of "any little, black, dried-up Frenchman." That is the way he thought of Philippe; and it was certainly well for the young American's peace of mind that he did not know that Molly and Judy always spoke of Philippe d'Ochtè as "the Adonis."

"Mrs. Brady, your good, strong, hot tea has done wonders for me. I am feeling so much better, I am going to take your advice and go for a long walk and not sit over the fire any longer."

He accordingly unwound his long legs, put the little blue letter with its health-giving postscript carefully in his breast pocket, (right over the spot of the vanished pain!) and went for one of his fifteen-mile tramps, humming sentimentally, "When the robins nest again, and the flowers are in bloom."

Mrs. Brady looked after him and smilingly shook her head: "He may say it's the tay, but there was some preschription in that bit o' blue paaperr I was ahfter destroyin' that was the pain-killer this toime for the poor young gintleman. Me prrivit opinion is that he, too, is a-missin' the swate eyes o' Miss Molly Brown!"

Professor Edwin Green came home from his long walk in an excellent frame of mind, happy and tired; but he was not too tired to write to Molly a letter that somehow she forgot to read to her mother and Judy.

CHAPTER X.

BOHEMIA.

What fun it was to be moving to their own apartment! Mrs. Pace was the only drawback to their happiness. She was very lugubrious and was sure they would find the ground floor damp, although it was explained to her that there was a good cellar under the studio and you went up several steps to the entrance. For a week before they left her, she would emit groans and shake her head sadly, saying: "I know it is a great mistake. These artists are notoriously careless and the place will be filthy, I haven't a doubt. And then the expense of keeping house is so great. Never mind, I shall hold your rooms in readiness for you and you can come back to them at any time."

"I beg you will do no such thing," said Mrs. Brown. "Of course we shall stay in the studio for six months, as we have rented it for that time. As for the dirt we are sure to find: you see Mrs. Bent is not an artist and she has the cleanest rooms I have ever seen."

But nothing convinced Henrietta Pace. She only knew that she was not to have the very pleasant boarders, so well connected, too, and so easy to please and courteous. Of course she blamed it on that very pert Miss Kean, who had defied her from the beginning; but what could one expect from a girl brought up in no place in particular, not even born in a fixed spot, (Julia Kean, you remember, was born at sea,) with a father who openly boasted of having a gizzard? And Mrs. Pace would give what Judy called, "one of her black satin sighs."

"Why should she dress in black satin all the time?" exclaimed Judy, after a particularly dismal dinner where Mrs. Pace had spent the time telling of all the misguided persons who had left her protecting wing and of the direful things that had befallen them. "The idea of any one as huge as she is wearing tight black satin! Why, I noticed two great square high-lights on her, measuring six inches across, one on her arm and one on her capacious bosom. In the latter, the whole dinner table was reflected. She should wear soft, loose things where no accenting high-lights could find a foothold."

"Oh, Judy, you are too delicious!" laughed Molly. "Who but you would notice the high-lights on your landlady's bosom, and then even the reflections in those high-lights? But weren't you amused at the 'unmerciful disaster that followed fast and followed faster' all the boarders that had not stayed at *Maison Pace*?

"One girl married a worthless art student and had to paint bathtubs for a living; one girl got lead poisoning in a studio where she was studying; one lady got her pocket picked on the Bois de Boulogne and one poor gentleman was lost at sea. Two of these calamities certainly could not have happened in this place. I'd defy anyone to get married here, even to a worthless art student, nor could one very well get lost at sea. I am glad we are to leave to-morrow and also glad that Elise O'Brien will not come until we are installed in the Rue Brea."

Molly had seen Frances Andrews several times since the recognition at the Opera, and had found her very agreeable but still peculiar, passionate and moody. She was extravagant in her affection for Molly and seemed eager to please Mrs. Brown. On the one occasion in which she had seen Judy when she called at the *Maison Pace*, she had been embarrassed and ill at ease with her and a little wistful, Molly thought.

She whispered to Molly on leaving: "I know Miss Kean despises me, but don't let her influence you. I am not as good as you think I am, but I am not half so bad as Miss Kean thinks I am. I got in wrong at Wellington and never could live down that scrape. Breaking the eleventh commandment is a terrible mistake: getting found out, I mean. I really did not do anything nearly so bad as lots of the other girls: Judith Blount, for instance. She did *mean* things and I never did. I was my own worst enemy and harmed no one else."

"Well, Judith Blount has 'come through,' as the darkeys say when they get religion, wonderfully well. It was the best thing that ever happened for her to become poor; and then she had such a wise little friend, Madeleine Pettit, who showed her how to work. You know I am your friend, Frances, and always did like you. You must not think Judy Kean does not, too. I am sure she has no reason to dislike you," and Molly bade her good-by with promises to come to call on her and her grandmother very soon.

But Frances was not mistaken about Judy's feelings for her. That young woman had a deep-seated dislike to the handsome, dashing Frances. "I don't trust her, Molly. She certainly did a dishonorable thing at college, and her eyes, although they are so beautiful, are a little shifty. I don't want to like her and I don't mean to, so there!"

The Browns' move from Boulevard St. Michael amounted almost to a flitting in the eyes of Mrs. Pace, as they departed while she was at market and had to leave their good-bye with Alphonsine for their respected landlady. The Marquise d'Ochtè sent her limousine to convey them to their new quarters, and knowing the habits of the redoubtable Henny, she deliberately had the chauffeur call very early for her cousins so that they could avoid the stormy good-bye she knew they would have to undergo.

They found the apartment shining and beautiful, everything swept and garnished, a fire burning in the big stove in the studio and a wonderful green bowl of chrysanthemums on the table. A little note was stuck in the flowers, bidding them welcome from the Bents and wishing them joy in the apartment where they had been so happy themselves.

"Aren't they the nicest people you ever saw," exclaimed Mrs. Brown. "The place looks as though it had been arranged for honored guests instead of just renters. I don't see how they could have slept here last night, eaten breakfast here, and left everything in such apple pie order. I almost wish Mrs. Pace could see it, just to keep her from feeling so sorry for us. Now let's unpack, put away our clothes, and make a list of what we need in the larder. When we go out for luncheon, we can do our purchasing."

"Of course we'll have dinner at home to-night. Elise gets in at four-thirty and Mr. Kinsella says he thinks there will be no doubt about her coming straight to us. He is to meet them at the station and intends to put the question immediately to Mrs. Huntington, and if her answer is favorable, he will bring Elise to us bag and baggage. So Pierce told me when he stopped in on his way to the art school to see if he could be of any service to us in the move. Oh, my mother, aren't we going to have a lovely time in our own little flat and away from that terrible dragon?" Molly kissed her mother and then flew up the steps of the balcony to the sleeping quarters that she and Judy were to occupy, just to peep out of the window into the court. Then she ran to the tiny kitchen. "I am itching to get to work on that little gas stove and see how it cooks," she exclaimed.

"Now, Molly, there is one thing I am going to put my foot down about: you are not to be working and cooking all the time we are in Paris. If this housekeeping is going to make you slave constantly, we will give it up and go back to Mrs. Pace. We will all share the work; the girls must do their part, too," and Mrs. Brown looked quite serious and determined.

"I promise, Mumsy, not to overwork but please let me do most of the cooking. I simply love to cook and I know Judy can't brew a cup of tea or boil an egg, and I fancy Elise has not had the kind of training that would make her very domestic. Of course, I'll be studying myself before so very long at the Sorbonne, and then I am afraid you will be the one to be overworked."

Just then there was a knock at the door: it proved to be the short-haired female artist from the adjoining studio. "I saw you had just moved in and I came to offer my assistance in settling you if you need me," she said in a voice singularly low and sweet for one of her very mannish appearance.

Her sandy hair was parted on the side and rather tousled, she had a freckled face and a turned-up nose, and a broad, good-natured, clever looking mouth. Her clothes were just as near being a man's as the law allowed: black Turkish trousers and a workman's blouse with paint all over the back, giving it very much the effect of the Bents' china press. Mrs. Brown and Molly looked at her wonderingly. She was a new and strange specimen to them. Their politeness was equal, however, to any shock and they thanked her for her kindness and asked her to come in.

"My name is Williams, Josephine Williams, commonly known as Jo Bill. Mrs. Bent told me of you and asked me to look after you until you got on to the ways of the Quarter and the tricks of the concierge. I thought I'd begin by asking you to afternoon tea to-morrow. I wish I could have you to-day but I've got a model posing for me and I must work every minute of daylight. I am going to get in the Kinsellas, our other neighbors, and Polly Perkins,—that is the man who lives in the court with us. He is not nearly such a big fool as he looks and talks."

"Is his name really 'Polly?'" asked Molly.

"Oh, no! He has a perfectly good man's name, but I am blessed if I remember it. Everybody calls him Polly. He is a cubist painter, you know; does the weirdest things and now has taken up a kind of cubist effect in sculpture; but you will see his things for yourself. I'd like to give him a good shaking and stand him in the corner. The poor fool can draw; made quite a name for himself at Carlo Rossi's and has a sense of color that even this crazy cult can't down. Goodness, how I am rattling on! I must fly back to my model who has rested long enough. You will come to-morrow, then? Please bring three tea cups with you," and the strange looking female strode off.

"Mother, isn't she funny? I like her, though, and think it will be grand to have tea with her and to meet 'Polly'."

"I like her, too," said Mrs. Brown. "She has such a nice, big, honest mouth. You know I never could stand little mouths. But, Molly, how on earth does she manage to wipe her paint brush on the back of her blouse and keep the front so clean? I wonder what kind of an artist she is."

"Maybe she is a futurist or a symbolist. Anyhow, she is very cordial and kind. I wish Aunt Clay could know that we are to have tea with a woman in trousers and a long-haired man."

The shops in the Rue Brea proved to be all that could be desired. A delightful little coffee, tea and chocolate shop was the first to be visited. It was no bigger than their tiled kitchen, but was lined with mirrors which gave it quite a spacious effect. The madame who presided was lovely and looked just like a cocoa advertisement in her cap and apron. They made their purchases of freshly ground Mocha-and-Java coffee and chocolate. The tea they had been warned against by the Marquise d'Ochtè. "Never get tea from a French shop or let a French person make it for you. Tea is beyond the ken of the French."

Then they went to a creamery, painted white inside and out as are all the creameries in Paris. There were great pyramids of butter ranged along the marble counter according to its freshness, with rosy girls deftly patting off pounds and half pounds, quarter pounds and even two sous' worth. Molly and her mother followed their noses to the freshest pyramid. It seemed to be just out of the churn and Molly declared that it made her homesick for Aunt Mary and the dairy at Chatsworth. They bought some of the delicious unsalted butter for dinner and left an order for a fresh pat to be sent in every morning for breakfast, also milk and cream and eggs.

Next came the grocery where they got their list of dull necessities in the way of flour, lard, salt, pepper, sugar and what not. Then the bakery, to order the little crescent rolls, *croissants*, to be sent in every morning and also to purchase a crusty loaf for dinner.

"Mother, smell that smell!" exclaimed Molly as they left the bakery. "What can it be? It is a mixture of all good cooking but I can't distinguish any particular odor."

Next to the bakery was a poultry shop, with every kind of winged creature hanging from hooks, inside and out: turkeys, ducks, chickens, geese, guineas, grouse, pigeons, partridges. In the back of the small, dark shop was a great open fireplace where logs of wood were blazing brightly, and in front of this fire were a series of spits, one over the other, stretching across the whole fireplace, all arranged to turn by a common crank. On these spits were stuck specimens of the different birds, and a fat, red-faced youth in white cap and blouse turned the spit and basted the browning fowls from a long, deep trough which caught all of the drippings. And so it happened that the turkeys borrowed delicacy from the pigeons; and the chickens, flavor from the wild duck, etc. And the gravy: Oh that gravy! All the perfumes of Araby could not equal it. The Browns were carried away by their discovery of this wonderful place. They immediately purchased a fine fat hen and monsieur, the proprietor, promised to have it roasted and sent hot to them by six-thirty.

"And please give us a whole lot of gravy, *beaucoup de jus*," demanded Molly.

The charming fat boy gave her a beaming smile and determined to take an extra quantity to the beautiful Americaine if he lost his job as spitter.

The dinner was a great success. Elise did come directly from the station as they had hoped she would, and she was so happy at being made one of the gay little crowd in the Rue Brea and so grateful to Mrs. Brown for taking her into her fold, that it made all of them glad to have her.

"Isn't it splendid to be able to loosen up and undress for dinner? It is especially fine when the dinner is so delicious," exclaimed Elise. "I am going to learn how to cook, if Molly will help me. Mamma never would let me go near the kitchen, and do you know I have never even seen any uncooked food except in shop windows and don't know a raw beefsteak from an old boot leg?"

"Papa says a French chef can cook up a boot leg with a sauce surprise that you couldn't for the life of you tell from the finest kind of steak. Now this roast chicken is the best I have ever tasted, with a gravy that has the squawk of the wild duck and the coo of a pigeon and — —" but here Judy stopped to help herself plentifully to the wonderful gravy and Molly finished out her speech for her:

"And the gobble of a turkey; and what attribute of the goose?"

The table in the studio, with its bowl of chrysanthemums, strips of Japanese toweling in lieu of a cloth, and odd blue china was very attractive. The china was odd in two senses of the word, as not a single saucer matched its cup and no two plates were of the same size. But what mattered that? Was not the coffee in the cups of the hottest and clearest and strongest? Was not the chicken and gravy, on the miscellaneous plates, food for the gods? Was not the rice, *à la*

New Orleans, a marvel of culinary skill? Where but in Paris could one find such crusty bread and delicious butter? The *salade Romaine* was crisp and fresh and Judy had made the salad dressing. It was her one accomplishment in the way of preparing food. She did it in great style and was always much hurt if any one else was given her job.

"Judy reminds me of Garrick and ought to make the dressing, anyhow," said Molly. "You remember what Sydney Smith said of him: 'Our Garrick's a salad, for in him we see, oil, vinegar, pepper, and mustard agree.'"

"Do you know the Spanish recipe for salad dressing?" asked Elise. "'A spendthrift for oil; a niggard for vinegar; a sane man for salt and a maniac for beating it.'"

Judy was proving her suitability by beating so vigorously and clicking so loudly with the fork, that a gentle knock on the door had to be sharply repeated before they were sure of it. There was a general scramble from the kimonoed crowd, who were not expecting a visitor at this hour. But Mrs. Brown, who wore a black China silk wrapper and was always presentable, went to the door where a small boy in a long white linen apron and a baker's cap stood with a huge flat basket on his head.

"Un gâteau pour Madame Brune."

"But we have not ordered a cake."

But the small boy was sure it was a cake for Mrs. Brown, and when the great flat basket was lifted from his head, there, in verity, was reposing a beautiful mocha cake with Mrs. Brown's name and address distinctly written on a card, but nothing else.

"An anonymous cake for Mumsy," laughed Molly. "Oh, you chaperone!"

There was another knock at the door, which this time turned out to be a bunch of violets apiece for the four ladies from Mr. Kinsella and a box of chocolates from Pierce.

"Why, this is a house warming, girls! What next? I wonder who sent the cake."

Mrs. Brown cut generous slices of that *spécialité* of Paris, with its luscious, soft coffee-flavored covering, hardly an icing, as it is too soft and creamy to be called that.

"*Ah, j'en ai jusque à la,*" said Judy, disposing of the last crumb of cake and making a motion of cutting her throat with her hand, "which in plain English means 'stuffed'. I am glad we can't eat the violets. Maybe after we move around a little we can hold some chocolates, but not yet, not yet!"

Mrs. Brown and Molly began to clear off the table, but they were forcibly held by Elise and Judy who insisted that the scullions' part was theirs.

"Mamma tried to make me promise to stand twenty minutes after meals for form's sake, I mean my own form," said Elise. "And what could be better than washing dishes for the complexion? A good steaming is what Mamma has said I need, as she declares I am so sallow, so I shall steam over the dishpan. Let's make a rule never to leave the dishes, no matter how tired we are. Mr. Kinsella says that when he and my father were sharing a studio here in Paris, when they were boys, they used to leave the dishes until they had used up all their supply; and then they would turn them over and eat off the bottoms of the plates. He says those careless ways are what disgust one finally with Bohemia."

"It was certainly kind of Mr. Kinsella to remember me, too, and send me a bunch of violets," said Judy as she wiped the cups Elise was washing.

"Mr. Kinsella is always kind," said Elise. "There never was such a thoughtful man. I feel so grateful to him, and I am going to work like a Trojan to let him see how I appreciate his interest in me." Elise blushed rather more than mere gratitude called for, and Judy thought that the dish water steaming was improving her complexion greatly already. She determined to wash next time herself and let Elise do the drying!

CHAPTER XI.

A STUDIO TEA IN THE LATIN QUARTER.

"The only thing that worries me in this delightful arrangement of co-operative housekeeping is the accounts," sighed Mrs. Brown at breakfast the next morning. "I am such a poor hand at arithmetic and a franc is so like a quarter that it is hard for me to remember it is only twenty cents; and a sou is so huge and heavy, I feel that it must be more than a cent. I pin my faith to a five franc piece which is like and is a dollar. I'd turn the money part over to Molly if she were not even worse than I am about it."

"Don't give it to me, please," begged Molly. "You know dear old Nance Oldham used to say I could do without money but I could not keep it."

"Well, Mrs. Brown, you should not be bothered to death about it, and I think we should elect a secretary and treasurer; and since there is no one here fitted to fill the place, I propose a new member to our club." Judy got up and reached from a high plate rack a funny, glazed Toby jug.

"I propose the name of Sir Toby Belch as a member of this club."

"I second the nomination and wish to offer an amendment to the motion," said Elise: "that the said Sir Toby be made secretary and treasurer of this association. All in favor of this amendment say 'Aye,' contrary 'No.' The ayes have it. Now are we ready to vote on the motion?"

The result was that Sir Toby Belch was unanimously elected and Mrs. Brown's duties were lightened. The plan was that every week the four members of the Co-operative Housekeepers' Association should put into Sir Toby a certain amount of money which would be drawn out for expenses as the occasion arose. If Sir Toby should get hungry and empty before the week was up, an assessment was to be made on all of the members and he was to be fed, even if it did happen to be between meals for him. If any member should be out of funds at the time, she could give an I. O. T. (I Owe Toby) which could be cashed when convenient.

"Dear lady, you shall not be worried," said Elise affectionately. "I believe this arrangement with Sir Toby will work beautifully."

And so it did. Sometimes Toby would get very lean and hungry and the few stray sous left in him would clink dismally against his ribs; and again he would be bursting with silver, paper and copper. Sometimes he would have to suspend payment until he could negotiate his I. O. T.'s., and sometimes when the week was up and all outstanding bills settled, he would be so affluent that he would treat the whole crowd to the theater or give a party to the friends in the Latin Quarter. Many a jest was made at his expense and sometimes Mrs. Brown and Judy, both of them able to quote Shakespeare at any point, would give whole pages of "Twelfth Night," impersonating the immortal Sir Toby and Sir Andrew Aguecheek and the naughty Maria.

Our friends went to many studio teas during their stay in Paris, but the first one with their erratic neighbor, Miss Jo Bill, they never forgot. Her studio was the size of their own but had no apartment attached. The hostess slept in a balcony, similar to the one Judy and Molly occupied, and her housekeeping and sleeping arrangements were much in evidence. Molly, going over ahead of the others to take the three tea cups requested, found Miss Williams washing her own five cups with their varied assortment of saucers and clearing off a table littered with papers and magazines, preparatory to placing the alcohol lamp, kettle and teapot thereon.

"Do let me help you," begged Molly. "Where is your tea towel? I can wipe the cups."

"Tea towel!" exclaimed Miss Williams. "Why, I don't possess such a thing! If the water is good and hot and clean, you don't need a towel. Just let the dishes drain. It is much more sanitary. Towels are awful germ harborers. But if you want to help, you might straighten up this table. Don't ask for a cloth or you will embarrass me."

Molly accordingly went to work and got order out of chaos in a short while. She piled the papers and magazines neatly on a shelf; emptied the teapot of its former drawing of leaves; washed and rinsed it; filled the kettle with fresh water; and replenished the alcohol lamp from a bottle of wood alcohol she found on the shelf.

"Well, if you aren't a peach, Miss Brown!" said the admiring Jo Bill. "I bet you are dying to go up on my roost and clear it out some. I was going to let it alone hoping to make it so interesting *en bas* that no one would glance up; but if you feel a calling to go up there and stir around a little, you are welcome."

Molly was itching to get her hands on the balcony, which reminded her of Mrs. Jellyby's closet, full to overflowing with every conceivable and inconceivable thing. The floor was strewn with coats, dresses and hats while the shoes were neatly hung on a row of hooks. Very pretty, well-shaped shoes they were, too, as it seemed Jo's feet were her one vanity.

"I never make up my bed, but just kick the covers over the dash board and let it air all day. Much more sanitary than tucking the germs in, giving them chance to multiply. You can make it up if you want to, though, since we are by the way of giving a party. Yes, hang up the dresses if you think it will improve the looks of things. I keep my shoes on the hooks so they can dry well and not be losing themselves all the time. I don't often need the dresses as I usually wear these painting togs. By Jove, speaking of dresses, I fancy I ought to put on one this afternoon! I wonder if your mother would think I was not showing her proper respect if I just put on a clean blouse and didn't try to get into one of those pesky dresses."

"Oh, don't dress up for mother, please! She would feel bad if she thought her coming would make any trouble for you, and besides, you hardly have time to do much; it is after five now," laughed Molly.

So Jo pulled off her workman's blouse and donned a clean one.

"Please tell me what makes you wipe your paint brushes on your back and how you manage it," asked Molly.

"What a question!" roared the amused Jo. "I wipe the brushes on the front of my blouses until it gets too gummy, and then I turn it hind part before. You and your mother must have thought I was some contortionist yesterday," and she extracted a hair brush from one of the shoes hanging on a hook and gave her tousled hair a vigorous punishment.

"Shall I put this tub out of sight?" asked Molly, picking up a great English hat tub.

"No, indeed, leave it there. I always put it where Polly Perkins can see it to shame him. You see he is as tidy as I am careless, but he leads an unhealthy, uncleanly life in spite of all of his pernickity ways, and I am really very sanitary and healthy in spite of all of my untidiness. In the first place, I take a cold bath every morning of my life and sleep in a hurricane of fresh air; and if my bed is in a mess, you notice my sheets are clean; while Polly is one of these once-a-weekers as to baths, and he is afraid of opening windows and letting in dust, and he makes up his bed the minute he gets out of it, animal heat, germs and all."

Molly was vastly amused and interested in her neighbor and her evident rivalry with the long-haired cubist, whom she now saw daintily picking his way across the court, in velveteen jacket and Byronic collar with the loose flowing tie common in the Latin Quarter. In his hand he held a stiff bouquet of red and yellow chrysanthemums, which, bowing low, he presented to Jo as she jerked the door open at his knock.

"The flower which you most resemble, I bring as an offering of — —"

"Stuff and nonsense! That's a nice thing to tell a girl: that she looks like a ragged chrysanthemum! I have brushed my hair, too, so your 'comparison is odious.' I have a great mind not to introduce you to Miss Brown just to pay you back for being so saucy."

But Mr. Perkins did not wait for the formal introduction. He came into the studio, his pasty face beaming, and gave Molly's hand a cordial shake. Then the others began to arrive: Mrs. Brown, Judy and Elise, Mr. Kinsella and Pierce.

"Polly, put the kettle on and we'll all have tea," sang Jo, and the obedient Mr. Perkins did her bidding. In a short while the water was boiling and the tea put to draw, and Jo produced from her cupboard a plate of Napoleons (that delicious pastry of Paris) and a *brioche*.

"Now, Jo Bill, that is mean to go have my kind of cake, too," exclaimed Polly Perkins fretfully. "You know I never have Napoleons at my teas because you call them yours, but *brioche* has always been mine; and when I have our neighbors in to my studio, what can I give them? I did not know you could be so sneaky."

Strange to tell, Jo took the repulse quite meekly and confessed that it was low, but there were not enough Napoleons at the *patisserie* and she had to fill out with something else.

"Please don't be cross, Polly. I got *brioche* because I know you like it so much. I like macaroons myself," and she helped the indignant cubist to a generous slice of his favorite cake and he was mollified.

The party was very gay. Jo proved to be a singularly tactful hostess and put them at their ease immediately. The tea was perfect.

"Where on earth do you get it?" asked Mrs. Brown as she accepted a second cup.

"Smuggle it," responded Jo. "Every time I go to California I bring enough back to run me for a year; enough for Polly, too. The custom house officials never hunt through my luggage for tea. They often remark that I am 'not the tea drinking type', but Polly, here, can't bring in a leaf of it without getting found out. He is a regular tea drinking type."

"Are you from California, too?" asked Molly, smiling at Polly and wondering if Jo's frankness hurt his feelings. But if it did he concealed his wounds remarkably well.

"Yes, indeed, Jo and I are from the same town. I have known her ever since she was a little boy. She is an awful clever sort and as kind and good as can be. I never mind her blague. We are the best friends in the world and she likes me as much as I do her. Have you seen her painting? She does the best and highest paid miniature work among the American artists in Paris. She has a very interesting way of working: paints everything big first and then in miniature. She says it keeps her from getting a sissy manner."

"I can't fancy Miss Williams with a sissy manner in anything," laughed Elise, who joined Molly and Mr. Perkins. "I want to see her things so much; and I do hope you will show us some of your work, Mr. Perkins. I hear you are of the new movement in art."

"Yes," said poor Polly sadly. "Jo hates me for it and refuses to think I am sincere or that there is any good in the movement, but I declare that she is the insincere one in not trying to see the good in the cubist movement. Jo is very hard-headed and conventional at heart, in spite of her pants."

The girls burst out laughing at this. The idea of Jo's being conventional was certainly absurd. Hard-headed she no doubt was.

"This will show you how stubborn she is: she pretends she does not remember my name. I don't mind her calling me Polly, but I do think she should address my letters to Mr. Peter Perkins and not Polly. I have known her ever since we were both of us babies and she must remember what my parents call me, even though she never did call me Peter herself," said the poor cubist who looked ready to weep.

Just then there was a diversion caused by a great knocking on a door in the court. It proved to be none other than Mrs. Pace.

"She has come to spy out the nakedness of the land," whispered Judy to Mr. Kinsella, who had been having a long talk with her. Pierce had had so much to say of this delightful young lady that his uncle was determined to make her acquaintance and find out if she were the kind of girl to be a help to his beloved nephew, or if there could be a chance of Judy's being the type that he had unfortunately come in contact with in his youth, causing so much disaster to his happiness. Judy was in her gayest mood and was enjoying herself hugely, and Mr. Kinsella seemed to find her quite as delightful as Pierce had led him to believe her to be. That young man was looking rather disconsolate since his uncle was occupying the place he coveted. He wandered over to where Elise was examining some of

Jo's miniatures. Elise, too, was a little wistful. She had looked forward with so much eagerness to meeting Mr. Kinsella again, and now on the first occasion when they might have had a real conversation, here he was spending the whole time laughing and talking with Julia Kean. She was glad of the diversion of Mrs. Pace's entrance, as it necessarily caused some cessation of what looked to her like a flirtation between Mr. Kinsella and Judy.

Enter, Mrs. Pace did, with a scornful sniff. After rapping sharply on the Browns' door and receiving no answer, she had made her way to the studio where the tea was being held. When Jo Bill opened the door, without waiting to tell her whom she was seeking, she swept into the room, "not like a ship in full sail," declared Judy to her companion, "but like a great coal barge in her shiny black satin and her huge jet bonnet."

Mrs. Brown introduced her to the members of the party with whom she was not already acquainted, but she acknowledged the honor only with a slight quiver of the stiff jet trimmings of her headgear.

"Well, Mrs. Brown! Is this what you left my house for?"

Mrs. Brown made no answer but Molly noticed that her nose was what Aunt Mary called "a-wucken'"; and she was wondering what would be the outcome of Mrs. Pace's rudeness, when Polly Perkins saved the day. He was taking tea to the uninvited guests at Jo's bidding. That young woman was totally oblivious and indifferent to Mrs. Pace's scornful attitude. She was Mrs. Brown's friend and she, Jo Bill, knew how to behave in her own house. Mrs. Pace was seated so that the last rays of the setting sun slanted through the window on her bonnet and the lighted lamp on the other hand shone full on her capacious chest, making the large square high lights of which Judy had made such merry jests. Polly handed her the cup of tea and slice of *brioche* and then backed away from her, standing with his eyes half closed and his hands clasped in adoration.

"Well, young man, what are you looking at me that way for?" snapped the irate Henny.

"Oh, Madame, you are so beautiful! You must pardon my raptures, but I am a cubist and you are exactly the type I am looking for to make myself famous withal. As I stand and gaze at you with my eyes half-closed, you present the most wonderful spectacle. I see a series of beautiful cubes, one on top of the other: black and gray, black and gray, and now and then where the light strikes, a brilliant white one. And oh, your *chapeau*! I can hardly wait to get to work on your portrait! You will sit to me, won't you?"

During this effusion, Mrs. Pace sat with a pleased smirk on her face. It had been many a long day since any one had called her beautiful, and no one had ever called her beautiful with such enthusiasm or wanted to paint her portrait. To be sure it was nothing but a small, pasty-faced, long-haired artist, but he was a man for all that, and his eyes were kind and earnest and his voice most appealing.

"I am a very busy woman," she answered gently, "but I will pose for you with pleasure, if it will help you in any way."

Her shiny ornaments trembled with emotion and she gave a sentimental sigh that broke the beautiful square high-light, so admired by Polly, into a dozen little ripples.

Mrs. Brown arose to make her adieux, taking Mrs. Pace with her to show the new quarters to the much softened lady. Mrs. Brown knew by the look in Judy's eyes that she would explode with laughter in a moment. Molly and Elise were bending over Jo's miniatures, their shoulders shaking. Pierce was standing in the middle of the floor with an alert expression as though he were in readiness to seize the lunatic, poor Polly, if he should become dangerous. Mr. Kinsella's composure was ominous of an outbreak. Jo Bill stood with arms akimbo and gazed at her former playmate, anger gradually gaining the ascendency over the amusement caused by his outspoken admiration of the ponderous and impolite Mrs. Pace.

As the door closed on the two ladies, Jo suddenly reached out, and grabbing Polly by his flowing tie, she boxed his ears soundly. "There, you goose, I've been wanting to do that for years!"

Polly received the chastisement with the utmost delight and actually seemed to look upon it as a form of caress from the enraged Jo. He whispered to Molly: "I believe Jo is jealous of the beautiful Mrs. Pace."

Mr. Kinsella asked Elise to take a walk with him that evening before dinner and they had the long talk that the girl had been eager for; and the little cloud of—not exactly jealousy, more envy of Judy's powers of attraction than jealousy, was dispelled for the time being.

CHAPTER XII.

THE GREEN-EYED MONSTER.

The winter went merrily on. Elise and Judy worked diligently at Julien's, the hard academic drawing being good for them and helping to counteract a tendency both had to rather slipshod methods. They gave only the morning to the school and in the afternoon looked at pictures or painted at home, if they could get a model among their acquaintances.

Judy made some charming memory sketches of the Paris streets. Seeing some bit that took her fancy, going or coming, she would burn to get her impression on canvas. She could hardly wait to get her hat and coat off, but would come tearing into the studio, pulling off her wraps as she came, hair flying, cheeks glowing, looking very like Brer Rabbit, Molly declared, when he ran down the hill with the six tin plates fer the chillun to sop outen; and the six tin cups fer the chillun to drink outen; the coffee pot fer the fambly; and the hankcher fer hisself, hollerin': "Gimme room, gimme room". They gave her room, all right, especially if her medium happened to be water color, as Judy was a grand splasher and spared neither water nor paint.

Elise was delighting in her steady work, the first she had ever been allowed to do. She lacked Judy's sense of color but on the other hand was very clever at sketching and getting a likeness, and had inherited her father's inimitable powers of caricature.

"Oh," sighed Judy, "if I could only get the people in my memory sketches to stand on their legs and seem to move as yours do, Elise, how happy I should be!"

"And I," said Elise, "would give anything if I could see and put on canvas the lovely colors that you can. I can't see anything but drab, somehow. It must be a somberness of disposition that affects my eyesight."

"But, Elise," broke in Molly, "you are not somber at all. You are full of jokes and *bon mots*."

"Oh, that is just my way here with all of you lovely, good, happy people. I am usually very dull and sober. Mamma says I can be the stupidest company in all the world, and I am sure she is right."

Elise had indeed blossomed in the congenial atmosphere in which she found herself for the first time in her life. Mr. Kinsella watched her eagerly, seeing many things about her to remind him of his old friend George O'Brien; and when the girl occasionally let drop some of the worldly cynicism that she had perforce learned from her mother, the sad look in his eyes would make her quickly repent her bitterness, and her endeavors to bring back his rarely sweet smile were almost pathetic in their eagerness. Mrs. Brown understood the girl thoroughly and did everything in her power to make her feel that she was one of the little coterie and a valued member; but Elise found it difficult to look upon herself as anything but an outsider. She was sensitively afraid of being in the way where Molly's and Judy's intimacy was concerned, and the girls often had to force her to join them on a lark unless Mrs. Brown was one of the party.

Pierce was "making good," as he expressed it, at the school. He had gone through several years of hard drawing at the League in New York, so decided that he could give his time to the painting that was to be his life's work. His uncle was delighted with his progress, and felt that his own youth was not lost at all but reincarnated in the glowing genius of his beloved nephew.

Molly was studying at the Sorbonne, where her Cousin Philippe d'Ochtè had duly installed her. It did not seem like studying, but more like going to the theater for several hours a day. The lecturers were so charming, so vivacious; their delivery was so dramatic, their gestures so animated. She drank in every word and found herself understanding French as she had never dreamed that she could.

She wrote on her stories when she was not attending the lectures. The Latin Quarter had given her several good plots and she was eager to work them out before Professor Green should put in his appearance, as she was anxious to let him see she had accomplished something during her Paris winter. That poor young man was still teaching the young idea how to shoot at Wellington and saw no hope of his release before March.

Kent Brown wrote cheerful letters from Kentucky. He was very busy in his chosen field of architecture and was learning French in a night class to fit himself for the Beaux Arts when he would finally be able to get to Paris. Aunt Clay was fighting the Trust vindictively as only she could fight and was dying hard, but Kent predicted that the end was near; and as soon as the suit was settled, he intended to take the first steamer abroad.

Mrs. Brown was not concerning herself in the least about her financial affairs. She felt sure that sooner or later she would realize on the sale of oil lands, and in the meantime the economy she and Molly were compelled to practice was rather exciting and interesting than annoying. Mrs. Brown had the happy faculty of adaptability, and living on Rue Brea she found there were many American students who were compelled to exercise the greatest thrift to exist.

Poor Polly Perkins was a sad example of the unproductive consumer. He had never earned a cent in his life and it looked as though he never would earn one, but still he stayed on in Paris, hoping against hope that his luck would change and that he could either sell a picture or that his cubist theories would become so popular that pupils would flock to him to sit at the feet of learning. He had a small monthly remittance from home that enabled him to pay his rent and by the strictest economy to clothe himself in the artistic garb of the Quarter (velveteen is fortunately very durable and not very costly); also to feed and partly nourish his far from robust little body. Mrs. Brown and Molly felt very sorry for Polly.

"He is such a sad little fellow," said Molly, "and he is very kind and good and takes Jo's teasing and bossing so patiently. He is really sincere about his art, and just because we can't see his way, we ought not to laugh at him. I believe Jo likes him a lot more than she knows she does. It nearly kills her for him to make himself ridiculous. I am crazy to see his portrait of Mrs. Pace. I do hope I can keep my face straight when he unveils it for us."

"Mrs. Pace declares it is wonderful. She told your Cousin Sally and me that it was a speaking likeness."

"Well, any likeness of Mrs. Pace would have to be a speaking likeness," laughed Molly.

Mrs. Brown and Molly were having one of their confidential talks, rather rare at that time, as Judy and Elise were usually at home when Molly was; or if mother and daughter did have a few moments alone, they were interrupted by callers: the Kinsellas or the d'Ochtès, Jo Williams or Polly Perkins or some of the new acquaintances they had made among the students.

"Mother, don't you notice a kind of sadness about Elise lately? She does not seem to me to be quite herself. Sometimes that old bitter way of talking gets hold of her and although she knows it pains Mr. Kinsella, she takes especial delight in giving vent to this satire when he is present. I am glad he has gone off to the Riviera for a change. She is devoted and grateful to him for influencing her mother to let her have the winter in Paris, but she has taken a strange way to show her gratitude in the last week or so.

"Did you see an almost noisy flirtation she was having with Philippe the last time we had all of them in to tea? She was not a bit like her sincere self, the natural, well-bred Elise that we all love so much, but more like her mother with her smart-set manner and flippant witticisms. I thought Cousin Sally was a little concerned about her precious Philippe. Cousin Sally is much more Frenchified in her soul than she dreams. I believe she is going to control the destiny of her son just as much as any mother in France."

Mrs. Brown smiled. She had an idea that she knew what Sally Bolling's plans for her son were: namely, her own Molly Brown. But since Molly herself had no idea of it, she was the last woman in the world to suggest it to her. She felt sure of her Molly, sure that no rank or wealth would influence her in choosing a mate (if choose one she must). She was confident that Molly liked Professor Green better than any man she knew, and that Philippe d'Ochtè with all his charm and good looks, wealth and position, did not appeal to her little daughter as did Edwin Green, the quiet, scholarly professor with no wealth at all. She had mentioned the professor only casually to her cousin, Sally d'Ochtè, as she did not feel it was incumbent upon her to speak of him as Molly's lover, since Molly herself did not consider him as one.

As for Philippe's heart, she did not think there was any danger of its being broken. She had carefully observed her young cousin and could see no sign of the languishing lover. That young man seemed to find difficulty in deciding which young lady he considered the most attractive. Molly was all that was lovely and sweet and delightful; Judy had a singular charm for him, with her vivacious manner and originality; Elise O'Brien evidently amused him and interested him greatly; and now a new star had come on his horizon: Frances Andrews, whom he had met at the Browns' and found very fascinating, a mixture of American and French. Philippe had, in truth, met too many charmers in too short a space of time and they had proved an embarrassment of riches, as it were.

His Cousin Mildred Brown knew what safety in numbers there was for him, and hoped he would not come to the conclusion that her Molly was the one of all others for him. Not that she did not like him. She was very fond of him and fully appreciated all of the d'Ochtè kindness to her and her little crowd of girls; but she had in a measure given her word to Edwin Green: that if he would not speak to Molly of his love for her for a year, he would find her daughter still unattached. She felt that she had done right in asking this of Professor Green. She was confident that she knew Molly's inmost thoughts and feelings, and that if she had any preference at all, it was for the young professor.

There were times when this anxious mother realized that one could not be too cocksure about the heart of anyone, even of one's own flesh and blood. Molly had noticed that Elise was not herself, and Mrs. Brown had noticed that none of her girls were quite themselves. For the last few days there had been a condition in the apartment in the Rue Brea of nerves at high tension; tempers a little uncertain; feelings a little tender. Mrs. Brown held her peace and endeavored tactfully to steer their little *ménage* safely over the shoals.

She thought she understood Elise. The poor girl was suffering with jealousy of Judy, who had plunged into an intimacy with the Kinsellas, uncle and nephew alike. She and Pierce would go on long tramps into the country and play a kind of game of memory sketches, seeing which one could bring home the greater number of impressions. Mr. Kinsella had become interested in their game and had joined them on one of their walks, becoming so fired with enthusiasm that he had actually tried to do some painting himself. He had been quite successful, considering the number of years that had passed since he had even so much as squeezed paint out of a tube. They had asked Elise to join them, but she had coldly refused. After those walks had become so popular with the trio, then it was that Elise had begun a rather half-hearted flirtation with Philippe d'Ochtè.

Judy was in one of her gayest and most irritating moods. "Getting ready for what she calls 'a Judy Kean scrape,' I am afraid," thought Mrs. Brown. "Our winter has been so peaceful and harmonious; but this mist will clear away soon, I know."

Judy seemed to realize that she was hurting Elise in some way but to be perfectly careless of the result. She never lost an opportunity to give Molly a dig about Frances Andrews, and when that young woman had come to the studio to tea, Judy had been very cold and almost rude to her. Molly, on her side, was a little distrait and listless and very touchy.

"What is the matter with my girls?" thought poor Mrs. Brown. "For the last week they have been like naughty children."

When Molly and her mother were having the little confidential talk recorded above, the elder lady did not realize that two American mails had come and that neither Judy nor Molly had received the bulky epistles that they usually did,—Judy one from Kentucky, and Molly one from Wellington. This was the cause of their unreasonable tempers. And had she but known it, on the other side of the Atlantic her own son Kent was eaten up with the green-eyed monster all because Judy had mentioned the name of Kinsella six times in her last letter! And he, Kent, had only that morning called his brother Paul "a conceited ass" because Paul had on a cravat to match his socks; and he had been equally unreasonable with a misguided waiter who brought him macaroni when he ordered spaghetti.

As for the dignified Professor Green, he had actually "hollered" at a poor freshman who had in reading some poetry pronounced "unshed tears" as though unshed were in one syllable. "'Unched tears', I could almost shed them," said the much-tried teacher; and all because a certain Molly Brown had a cousin Philippe who was kind enough to see that she heard all the lectures worth while at the Sorbonne.

Mrs. Brown decided to take Molly into her confidence and divulge to her her ideas concerning Elise and Mr. Kinsella. Molly was astonished and delighted.

"Oh, mother, how wise you are and how blind I am! I realize now how Elise must have suffered and all for nothing. I just know Mr. Kinsella adores her. I see it all. He went off just because he thought Elise was serious about Philippe and he could not stay to see it. How I wish he would come back and it could all be set right, and dear Elise could make up to him for all the suffering her mother caused him! I do wish I could put a flea in Judy's ear and she would behave."

"But you must not do that, my dear," said Mrs. Brown. "That would not be quite fair to Elise. You see it is only surmise on our part."

"Right as usual, mother, but it is going to be hard to see things going wrong when a word would right them. Judy means no harm and is really doing nothing. She takes long walks with Mr. Kinsella and Pierce, and Mr. Kinsella delights in Judy's frankness and originality. He likes to be with her, but as for thinking of her in any other light than as Pierce's playmate,—I don't believe it has entered his head."

"I am sure it hasn't; but Elise has had very few friends and has been brought up in such a selfish world, that she is perhaps prone to see the wrong motive. Molly, do you feel well? I have fancied you were a little pale lately and not quite so enthusiastic as usual."

Just then there was a knock on the door and the concierge's little son entered, bringing a stack of mail. One from Wellington was on top, and Molly was able truthfully to tell her mother that she never felt better in her life.

CHAPTER XIII.

A JULIA KEAN SCRAPE.

One day in late February when there was a faint hint of spring in the air, on the way to the art school Judy said to Elise:

"I am dead tired of drawing from a model indoors. I've a great mind to cut the whole thing and do something desperate. I know the sap is rising in the trees and the color is getting wonderful and more wonderful every day. I believe I'll go on a high old lonesome to the country, take my sketch box, pick up some luncheon where I happen to land and have a general holiday. Why don't you come, too?"

"Thank you, no. If I should go, too, it would not be a high old lonesome for you; and then, besides, I am so interested in the model this week," said Elise.

She did not say that she half expected Mr. Kinsella back that afternoon and could not bear to be out of Paris when he returned. Mr. Kinsella had been off on a three weeks' jaunt, and during his absence Elise had taken herself severely to task for her behavior to him and to everyone. She had reasoned herself into seeing how absurd her jealousy was toward Judy, and when Mr. Kinsella should return, he was to find a much chastened Elise.

"But, Judy," continued Elise, "if you do go, you will skip a criticism from the master; and then, isn't it a little imprudent for you to go out to the country all alone?"

"Oh, I am glad to skip a criticism from old C— —, he is such an old fogy. All he can say is: '*Ça va mieux, mademoiselle, ça va mieux!*' As for being imprudent going to the country alone, why, I am surely big enough, old enough and ugly enough to take care of myself," and Judy made a face and assumed a militant air.

"Well, you are ridiculous enough to carry through any project," laughed Elise. "And where will you go, you big, ugly, old thing?"

"Oh, not far. St. Cloud, perhaps. I fancy I'll be back before you get home. I am not so crazy about being by myself when I once get there. I am a gregarious animal when all is told. Good-by, my love to old C— —," and Judy swung off, determined to take one of the little boats to St. Cloud.

It was a glorious day. The water of the Seine was clear and blue; the little boats were puffing up and down; the fishermen lined the walls and patiently and diligently cast their hooks. Judy stood on the Pont Neuf glad she was living; glad she was in Paris and had eyes to see it and ears to hear it; glad of her truancy; gladdest of all when one old fisherman actually caught a fish and she was there to behold it. She had been told that none were ever caught, that the fishermen sat there day after day, year after year, with never a reward for their patience. She wandered up the quay, not certain whether she would take a boat to St. Cloud or go to the station and catch a train for Versailles. As she loafed along, an ogling old man joined her and with voluble protestations assured her of his admiration of her beauty. Judy gave him a withering glance and, quickening her pace, soon left him far behind.

"That is exactly what Papa warned me against," she thought. "He said: 'Never loaf along the streets when you are alone. Have some business to attend to and attend to it and no one will have anything to say to you.' I must assume some business if I have it not."

She accordingly put on an air of great purpose, grasped her sketching kit very firmly, and went and got on a little "penny puff puff" that was just starting out for Sèvres and St. Cloud.

St. Cloud was beautiful, indeed. The sap was rising in the trees and a few buds were showing their noses on bush and shrub. There was a haze over everything like a tulle veil, and Judy had an idea if that would lift, she could catch a glimpse of spring. She remembered that these groves were the ones that Corot loved to paint and indeed the effect was very much that obtained by that great artist: a soft, lovely, misty atmosphere, with vistas through the trees, and an occasional glimpse of shining water. Judy made several tiny "postage stamp" sketches. "Taking notes from nature," she called it.

"I wish some nymphs would come dancing out now," she exclaimed. "Corot could call them up at any time, and why not I? 'I can call spirits from the vasty deep. And so can I, and so can any man; but will they come when you do call them thus?'" No nymphs came, but a wedding party appeared, the buxom bride dressed in white with a long veil and wreath of artificial orange blossoms, the groom in dress coat, gray trousers, and red cravat.

St. Cloud is a famous place for wedding parties of the *petit bourgeois*, and Judy felt herself to be very fortunate to witness this first one of the spring. The bride's dress looked rather chilly for February although it was such a warm, sunny day; but through the coarse lace yoke it was easy to see that the prudent young woman had on a sensible red flannel undershirt, and as she turned around and around in the mazes of the dance, with the ecstatic groom, an equally sensible gray woolen petticoat was in plain view. A hurdy-gurdy furnished the music and the greensward was their ballroom floor. Everyone danced, old and young, fat and lean.

Judy sat entranced and beat time with her eager feet. It was such a good-natured crowd. The groom's mother danced with the bride's father, and the bride's mother danced with the groom's father. Everyone had a partner and everyone seemed to feel it to be his or her duty as well as pleasure to dance as long as the hurdy-gurdy man could grind out a tune. The fat mother of the bride (at least Judy thought she must be her mother from a similarity of gray woolen petticoats) sank on the bench almost into the wet sketch with the Corot effect, and made speechless signals that she could proceed no farther. Her disconsolate partner was not nearly through with his breath or enthusiasm. He was as lean as his partner was fat and had not so much to carry as the poor mother of the bride. He took two or three steps alone, kicking out his long legs like a jumping-jack, and then he made a sudden resolve. Coming over to Judy, he took off his hat, pressed it to his starched shirt bosom, made a low bow and asked her to take pity on a poor old man who would have to dance alone, as dance he must, unless she would be his partner.

Impulsive Julia Kean found herself on a terrace at St. Cloud, spinning around like a dancing dervish. She, with her partner, danced down the whole wedding party; even the untiring street piano gave up, and their last spin was taken without music. The good-natured revelers applauded loudly; and some of them congratulated her on her powers of endurance; and the flattered *bon père* declared that in his youth he had been able to dance down three charming partners but he had never had the pleasure of dancing with a young lady with the endurance of the English miss. With that, he heard a scornful "Bah" from his good wife, who berated him for his stupidity in not knowing *l'Americaine* from *l'Anglaise*.

"An English lady would be scornful of our kind, but an American would not be so particular, blockhead?" And the large grenadier of a woman, looking like one of the commune, gave his ear a playful tweak.

"My wife is jealous, mademoiselle. She was ever thus," said the lean dancer; and all the company roared with delight at his wit. Then the hurdy-gurdy started up a brisk polka. Judy was claimed by the grinning groom, and once more her endurance was put to the test. For the honor of her country, she was glad of her athletic training and record at Wellington. The bride was dancing with her new father-in-law, Judy's former partner, and it was recognized at the beginning that this was to be fight to the finish between the two couples.

"Breathe through your nose and save your wind," she whispered to her partner, who was puffing like a porpoise and showed signs of giving in. The others had one by one succumbed to fatigue and were now sitting in a more or less exhausted state on the various benches, noisily applauding the endurance of the spinning couples and betting on their favorites.

The groom was not the man his father was, but he had youth in his favor; and Judy had the advantage of the bride in lightness and training. The old father was beginning to look grim and haggard, and the bride very hot, with her red flannel shirt showing in splotches through her moist wedding finery. Judy's soul was filled with compassion. This was the bride's day and no honor should be wrested from her. If the husband scored one on her to-day she might never catch even, and he might hold the whip hand over her for the rest of their married life. As for the old man, it was hard enough to be old and have young ones usurp your place.

Judy made a sudden resolve to let her opponents win. She was the stronger member of their team and knew if it had not been for her endurance, the young man would have given in long ago; so assuming a shortness of breath that she did not really feel, she slid from her partner's flabby embrace and sank on a bench by the side of the bride's mother, just a second before the old man and his daughter-in-law flopped in an ignominious heap on the grass.

Being tired and victorious is a very different thing from being tired and beaten, so the fallen pair were soon restored. The groom picked up his lady-love and bestowed a burning kiss on her panting mouth, (just to let her know there was no hard feeling,) and Judy, remembering she had in her shirtwaist in lieu of a missing button, a tiny enamelled American flag, went forward and pinned it on the lapel of the old man's coat, and making a low curtsey, said:

"A tribute from America to France!"

There was much applause. Judy was urged by all present to stay with them all day, but she had decided to take a train at the nearby station for Versailles and get her luncheon there, so she bade them good-by. Gathering up her sketches and sliding them into the grooves in the back of her kit, she left the gay throng and soon got a local to Versailles.

On reaching Versailles, she did not go into the palace but wandered in the park, stopping to feed the carp in the pond with some gingerbread she had bought from a red-cheeked old woman. These carp are large and fat and lazy, lying at the bottom of the pool, moving their tails almost imperceptibly and opening and shutting their eyes with such a bored expression that Judy had to laugh. There is a rumor that they are the same carp that Marie Antoinette used to feed; certainly they are very old and very tired. Judy remembering this legend of the carp, began to think of poor Marie Antoinette and decided to go over to the Trianon. The poor misunderstood queen had always been one of Judy's favorites. She walked along under the trees in a brown study musing on the fortunes of that royal lady.

Suddenly she rubbed her eyes. Was she dreaming or was she crazy? The Trianon was before her and on the terrace was Marie Antoinette herself dressed as a shepherdess and leading a beautiful woolly lamb by a blue ribbon. Accompanying her was a pretty maid of honor dressed as a milk maid with a pail in her hand and a three-legged stool under her arm. The Count d'Artois, gay, handsome, debonair, met them and held them in conversation, then the grave, sedate Monsieur, as the elder of the two brothers of King Louis XVI was styled, approached, and with him was our own Benjamin Franklin, dressed in sober brown.

"Where am I? What can it mean? I am wide awake, and that is as certainly Benjamin Franklin as that I ate Quaker Oats every morning for breakfast at Wellington. But who is this madman?"

A furious person in shirt sleeves came tearing across the terrace. In plain American he berated Marie Antoinette, the grave Monsieur, d'Artois and even the dignified Franklin, and, strange to say, they took it very amiably. True, the spoiled Marie pouted a bit, but Franklin, with a vile Cockney accent, said:

"I saiy, wot's your 'urry? The negative hain't spoiled none. Hold 'Press the Button' hain't in his box."

"Moving picture actors," exclaimed Judy. "What a sell!"

She sat and watched them for some time, amused by the vociferous manager, who did not hesitate to swear at the royal Louis XVI, who came into view, forgetting to show the bunch of keys he was supposed to have fashioned with his own kingly hands.

The day had been full of adventure and in consequence a great success in Judy's eyes. She was tired of the humdrum of the last few weeks and her soul thirsted for excitement. "I do wish Molly had come. How she would have enjoyed the thrill of seeing Marie Antoinette in her own setting of the Trianon; but if I had been with anyone, I am sure the dear old dancing father would never have asked me to dance and I should have missed that delightful experience of being one of a wedding party at St. Cloud.

"Molly is a little hurt with me, anyhow, because I have been rather nasty about Frances Andrews. Frances is improved but I have not had the courage to tell Molly I am sorry, and knowing I am wrong makes me ruder than ever to Frances. As soon as I get back to town I am going to 'fess up. Frances is off on a trip with her grandmother, but when she comes back she will find me as polite as a basket of chips. Suppose Molly had turned her back on me when I got into all of those mix-ups with Adele Windsor! I don't know whether I would have had the backbone to go through with the senior year or not if it had not been for Molly. Frances is certainly much more of a lady than Adele Windsor and she has never done a thing to hurt me. I am going to try to be good. I know dear Mrs. Brown will be glad.

"I fancy that dear lady has had some worried moments lately. Elise has got over her dumps and is behaving like a rational human being, and I am the only one who has not reformed. I am going to get my lunch and go right back to Paris and tell them what a brute I am and how good I am going to be. Kent would hate me for worrying his mother, and he despises meanness in anyone."

Judy accordingly went to a little café near the station and ordered a good luncheon, which took almost all of the change she had in her pocket; but her ticket back to Paris, which was only a few sous, was all that she needed so she did not let her finances worry her. She still had a bag with a big slab of gingerbread in it. This she determined to leave at the café as it was a cumbersome parcel, but the *garçon* ran after her with it and she thought it a simpler matter just to take it along, not knowing that the time would come when she would look upon that gingerbread as her preserver. Inquiring at the station, she found there would not be a train back to Paris for about half an hour and so, after buying her ticket, she determined to take a walk in the Versailles grounds rather than spend the time waiting.

She chose a rather unfrequented path leading to the lake and walked slowly for Judy, who was ever quick in her movements; but the day was beginning to drag a little. She was, as she had told Elise, a gregarious animal, and a whole day of her own company was beginning to pall on her. She sat down on a bench. Along the path came a typical Boulevardier, a very much over-dressed dandy, with shiny boots and hat, lemon colored gloves, waxed black mustache and beard, and all the manner of a "would-be-masher." How Judy hated his expression as he ogled her! But she thought utter disregard of him would discourage him, so she assumed a very superior air and looked the other way. The Frenchman was so certain of his powers of fascination that he could not believe her manner to be anything but coy, so he sank on the bench by her side and began in the most insinuating way to praise her beauty and style, her hair, eyes and mouth. The girl was furious, but determined to say nothing, hoping by her scornful silence to drive off her admirer. He persisted, however, in his unwelcome attentions.

"*Peut-être madamoiselle* does not schpick *Français*. I can *parler* a leetle Eenglesh, *mais pas beaucoup*." Judy rose from her seat, overcome with indignation and a slight feeling of fear.

"I know he can't hurt me," thought the girl, "but he can make things very disagreeable and embarrassing for me."

The place seemed singularly lonesome and desolate. The bright sun had gone behind a cloud and a sharp breeze had sprung up. There was not a soul in sight and the station was at least a five minutes' walk distant. As she hurried off, the man picked up the bag, from the top of which gingerbread was protruding, and followed her.

"You have forgot your *gouter*, *cherie*. Do you like puddeen very much, my dear?"

Judy seized the bag of gingerbread that she seemed unable to lose, and a sudden remembrance of her talk with Elise came to her: "I am big enough, old enough and ugly enough to take care of myself." She thought if it was beauty that he was admiring she would cure him fast enough. She grabbed the slab of soggy brown cake from the bag and crammed about six inches of it into her mouth, the rest of it sticking out in a manner far from dainty. It had the desired effect. The fastidious Frenchman was completely disgusted. He immediately stopped his pursuit, exclaiming with a shrug: "*Ah quelle betise!*"

When Judy arrived at the little station a train was on the track, and without waiting to ask any question of the guard, since she had her ticket, she jumped into a second class coach from which someone had just alighted, slammed the door shut, sank back on the cushions and burst out crying. Crying was something in which Judy was not an adept and only a few tears came, but she felt better because of them. Then she settled herself for a pleasant, if short, trip to Paris. There was no one in the coach with her, for which she was very thankful.

"I'd hate for anyone, even a Frenchy, to see me blubber. Oh, how I should have liked to hit that man a good uppercut on the jaw! I shall crow over Molly. I did as much with a piece of gingerbread as she did with a tennis racket when she floored the burglar who was after Mildred Brown's wedding presents. This looks like a long trip to Paris. We should be getting there by this time. We are going mighty fast for a local. Oh, these beastly foreign trains where they hermetically seal you and you can't ask a question until you get to a station."

The train slowed up but did not stop. They passed a village and then another and another. The country was not familiar to Judy. She read "Rambouillet" on a passing station, and then the fact became clear to her that she was on the wrong train, going from Paris instead of towards it.

"Rambouillet is at least twenty miles from Paris. Judy Kean, you idiot, you idiot, you idiot!"

Judy was in truth on the Chartres express with six sous in her pocket, left after she bought her ticket to Paris; and the one piece of jewelry she might have converted into enough cash at least to telegraph her friends, was pinned on the coat of that crazy old dancing fiend.

CHAPTER XIV.

COALS OF FIRE.

A furious, vociferous guard bundled Judy out of the coach, when on arriving at Chartres the door was unlocked. She showed her ticket to Paris and endeavored to explain her mistake and situation, but he was almost inarticulate with rage at her for having "stolen a ride" as he expressed it; and now she could look out for herself. It was none of his affair. She went into the waiting room to find out when the next train to Paris was due. She debated whether or not she should tell the ticket agent of her trouble and see if he could pass her back to Paris, but his appearance was so forbidding and his eyes so fishy that she could hardly make up her mind even to ask the time for the train. She made out from a bulletin that it was not due until ten at night. That would land her in Paris at midnight. In the meantime, she must raise enough money to pay for her ticket and hire a taxi when she got to Paris. She must also manage to send a telegram to Molly.

"Julia Kean, you have always thought yourself pretty clever and this is the first time in all your life you have had really and truly to depend on yourself. Now let's see what you can do. First thing, I warn you not to sniffle and get sorry for yourself. If you do, the game is up. Suppose I can't raise the spondulicks in time for the ten train! Maybe I had better drop a postal to Molly with some of my six sous so she can get it first pop in the morning."

This she accordingly did. She found a tobacco shop where stamps and postal cards were sold and mailed a piteous appeal to Molly. She then found a telegraph office and wrote a telegram to be sent collect, but the hard-hearted operator refused to send it unless she prepaid it, and that she could not do. Her French deserted her whenever she thought of explaining her situation to anyone. She kept her eye open for Americans or even English, but not a sign of a foreigner did she see.

"I might have raised a little money on the American flag if I only had not been so smart-Alec and given it to that old man. I wonder what possessed me to eat such an expensive lunch at Versailles! I fancy it was my virtuous resolve to be nice to Frances Andrews that made me feel like treating myself. Thank goodness for the gingerbread! I won't starve, at least," and she hugged to her faint heart the remains of her preserver in time of peril and need.

Whom should she see approaching at this juncture but Frances Andrews and her grandmother? Judy's first feeling was one of delight; but she remembered how rude she had been to Frances and her resolve to be nice to her, and felt if she should be cordial now there could be but one interpretation for Frances to put on it, and that would be: she had an "axe to grind."

She bowed coldly and Frances returned the salutation, but she stopped her to ask if the Browns were in Chartres, too.

"No, I am here alone," said Judy with great nonchalance, "I bid you good afternoon," and she walked on, trying to keep her back from looking dejected.

"Grandmother, there is something the matter with Miss Kean and I feel as though I should find out if she needs help," said Frances, gazing after Judy until she turned the corner.

"Nonsense, my child. She is a bad-mannered piece. I have an idea I know why she is in Chartres. I believe it is a runaway match between her and that dark, middle-aged man we met at the Browns' tea. I caught a glimpse of him at the hotel at déjeuner to-day. Kinsella is his name. I could not quite place him but knew his face was familiar. You keep out of it. It is none of your business if persons choose to make fools of themselves," and the irate old woman clutched her granddaughter's arm and dragged her along.

"There is no use in trying to stop me, Grandmother. She is Molly Brown's friend, and while she is horrid to me, I am going to see if she needs my help for Molly's sake. You can get back to the hotel alone; if you can't, just call a cab," and Frances whisked off, leaving her aged relative fussing and fuming in the street.

With all of Judy's acting, Frances had seen that she was excited about something and she certainly had not the air of one coming to meet a lover. The day in the country had not been conducive to tidiness. Judy's hair was blown, her collar and shirtwaist were rumpled, her shoes dusty and the tears in the train had left a smudge on her cheek.

On turning the corner, Judy had discovered a pawnbroker's shop. "That is where people in books go when they are hard up, so that is where I am going," she thought.

It was kept by a benevolent looking old Jew, and benevolent he may have been, but Judy soon found out, as she expressed it, "He was not in business for his health."

She asked him what he would give her for her sketching kit. It was a very attractive and expensive little box, with a palette, a drawer full of color tubes, a partition with sliding panels for sketching and a tray of brushes. He sniffed with disgust and said, "Two francs."

Judy's heart sank. Forty cents for a box that cost at least ten dollars, counting the tubes of expensive colors! But she remembered that at a pawnbroker's you can redeem your belongings, so she decided to take the forty cents and send a telegram with it.

"There are some sketches in here that I should like to dispose of, too, but they are more valuable than the box," she added slyly, having an instinct that she must meet the old man on his own ground and cry up her wares. "Be careful! The paint is not quite dry on them."

She slid the panel with the Corot effect out of the back of the box and held it out to the ancient Shylock. He adjusted his horn spectacles on the end of his long nose and holding the sketch upside down, viewed it critically.

"Ah, very pretty, very pretty; two francs fifty for it; but I want to buy it, not to be redeemed. Any more?" and the dealer stretched out his eager hand.

Judy had two more which she got a franc apiece for, making in all six francs fifty, one dollar and thirty cents, enough to get her back to

Paris traveling third class, since she already had her ticket from Versailles to Paris.

"I can't telegraph to Molly, though, I haven't enough money," she thought sorrowfully. "I hate to think how worried all of them will be. I should have told Frances about my predicament, but somehow I could not bring myself to ask a favor of her when I have always been so nasty to her."

The old pawnbroker could hardly wait for Judy to get out of his shop to begin his work on the sketches, converting them into perfectly good, authentic antiques. The Corot effect he put by a very hot fire, not quite hot enough to scorch it but hot enough to dry it very quickly and bake it, so it was covered with innumerable tiny cracks. Then he took some shellac, dissolved in alcohol and mixed with a little yellow ochre, and sprayed this all over the sketch. The result was remarkable. He then slipped it into a heavy gilt frame (still upside down), and displayed it in his window with the price mark: forty francs, without the frame.

Judy, feeling a little sad over her beloved sketching kit but jubilant over her financial success, started down the street and bumped right into Frances Andrews, who was eagerly searching for her. Judy made a sudden resolve to be nice to Frances from that time on. Frances spoke first:

"Miss Kean, I do not want to intrude on you, but I want you to feel that you can call on me to serve you in any way in my power. We are both of us Molly's friends and somehow I have a feeling that you need help of some sort."

"Frances—I am not going to call you Miss Andrews—I have been in a pickle but since I met you and your grandmother on the street I have come into a fortune of a dollar and thirty cents, so my troubles are about over. I am going to tell you all about it, but first I want to tell you that I am sorry I have been so rude and hateful and cold to you. I have been out in the country alone with my conscience all day and determined to be a nicer, sweeter girl and to apologize to you and to Molly; but I got on the train at Versailles going away from Paris instead of towards it, and landed here in Chartres with only six sous in my purse. When I met you on the street, I felt if I told you how sorry I was that I had been so studiedly mean, you would think I had a change of heart because I wanted something out of you; but now that I have earned enough to get back to Paris, you can't think that. You show yourself to be generous-hearted and kind by coming back to look me up after I was so unbearable to you and your grandmother. You have heaped coals of fire on my head."

As the girls talked they had come near the hotel where Frances and her grandmother were stopping.

"Well, Judy—I can't call you Miss Kean ever again—I think you are simply splendid and worthy to be Molly's friend and I do thank you for what you have said. Now you must promise to have dinner with grandmother and me at the hotel and you can come up to my room and rest." And be it said right here that Frances proved herself to be very much of a lady for not adding "and wash your face," for Judy's face was ludicrously dirty. "Grandmother said she thought she saw Mr. Kinsella at the hotel."

"What, Uncle Tom? How splendid!" exclaimed Judy, realizing that her troubles were at last over.

Mr. Kinsella was sitting on the piazza as they approached. He jumped to his feet and hurried down the steps. Explanations were soon over and the kind gentleman took affairs in his own hands. The plan was that all of them should take the ten o'clock train back to Paris. Mr. Kinsella went off immediately to telegraph Mrs. Brown of Judy's whereabouts.

The friends in Rue Brea had begun to be very uneasy about Judy. All they knew was what Elise could tell them of the girl's sudden determination to cut the art school and spend the morning in the country. Dark came and no Judy. Pierce Kinsella was called into consultation and could throw no light on the subject. Jo Williams consoled them greatly by saying:

"Don't worry about Judy Kean. She is the kind to light on her feet."

So she was, but worry they did. Elise reproached herself for not going with her. Pierce wished his uncle had come back as he had half hoped he would that afternoon. They were a very disconsolate crowd. It was seven o'clock and no clue to their beloved friend. A knock on the door: *"Une dépêche pour Madame Brune!"*

"A telegram, a telegram!" Mrs. Brown's hands trembled so that Pierce had to open it for her.

"Why, it is from Uncle Tom! 'Miss Judy Kean safe in Chartres with me. Will arrive in Paris at midnight. T. Kinsella.' That's all."

"Well, of all things! What is Judy doing in Chartres?" exclaimed Molly and her mother in one breath.

Elise, her face crimson and eye flashing, burst out with: "Lighting on her feet, evidently, like the cat she is!" She covered her face with her hands and fled to her room.

Pierce looked mystified, the Browns both distressed, and Jo Williams snorted: "So that's what is the matter!"

In the meantime, Judy was having a splendid time. Knowing her friends in Rue Brea were no longer worrying about her, she gave herself up to enjoyment. Mr. Kinsella dined with the three ladies and Judy kept them in a gale with the description of her day of adventure. That young woman never did things by halves, and she was now engaged in fascinating Frances and her grandmother with as much spirit as she had formerly exercised in insulting them. The old lady was completely won over and Frances was too glad to have Molly's friends like her not to want to let bygones be bygones.

After dinner Mr. Kinsella redeemed the sketching kit, paying twenty per cent. interest for the loan. He saw the Corot in the window, where it looked very genuine in its old gilt frame. He offered the man forty francs for it, including the frame and the bargain was clinched in short order. They made very merry over this, and Judy descanted on the genius that could paint a picture that looked just as well upside down as rightside up.

"You see the bit of sky in the upper right corner makes very good water when turned over, and the water in the lower right corner makes a dandy sky."

Mr. Kinsella wrapped his prize up very carefully and said he intended to fool Pierce with his find of a genuine old master.

CHAPTER XV.

MR. KINSELLA'S INDIAN SUMMER.

The next morning Molly arranged a tray with a very inviting breakfast and took it to Elise's room. She found her still in bed, looking very woebegone and wistful.

"Oh, Molly! You should not spoil me so. I was getting up, at least thinking about getting up. I did not sleep very well at first and towards morning went off into such a deep slumber that I could not wake up," exclaimed the girl.

"I love to spoil people, besides you are always the energetic one and might for once be allowed a little morning snooze. I hope Judy and I did not keep you awake. She had so many adventures to tell me that it was two o'clock before we quieted down. She got into the wrong train at Versailles and was landed at Chartres with only six sous in her pocket. With part of this wealth she sent me this postal which has just come, fearing when she sent it that she might have to spend the night in Chartres. Only read it and see what a plight she was in," said Molly, handing the smudgy, pencilled postal to Elise.

"Dearest Molly: Here I am alone in Chartres, where as far as I can see there is not one friendly soul. Got on the wrong train at Versailles. Have five sous left after buying this postal but am not discouraged. Will try to sell my sketch box. Have no jewelry but have enough gingerbread to keep me from starving. Will sit up all night in station. Get Pierce to come for me in morning and bring my toothbrush. Will be home soon as I get some money. Judy."

"Guess whom she met first in Chartres: Frances Andrews and her grandmother! Then Mr. Kinsella. But before she did anything, she sold her sketches for enough to get her here third class on the train. She has made up with Frances and is now as enthusiastic about her as she used to be down on her. What a Judy she is, anyhow!

"Mr. Kinsella has been here twice this morning to ask if he could see you. He is afraid you are ill because you are sleeping so late. He told me to beg you not to go to the art school this morning but to take a holiday with him. He says this wonderful weather will have to break soon, as it is too unseasonable to last."

Molly's heart was filled with joy to see the effect her words had on her friend.

Elise finished the last crumb of *croissant* and drained the last drop of coffee. "It does seem best to take advantage of the good weather for a little outing, and, besides, the model we have is thoroughly uninteresting this week."

Elise bounced out of bed and Molly noticed that all trace of her bad night had left her face. Elise did not remember that only the day before she had thought the model too interesting to think of cutting work for the day!

Judy, peeping from her balcony where Molly had been spoiling her, too, with breakfast in bed, saw Mr. Kinsella and Elise start off on their jaunt.

"Molly, Molly!" she screamed. "I have made a most wonderful discovery: Elise and Mr. Kinsella are—are—well, seekin'! As they went off just now there was something in the way he looked at her and she looked at him that made me know it's so."

"Well, old mole, if you had not been as blind as a bat you would have seen that all winter. I was dead to tell you, so you would not make Elise so jealous of you, but mother would not let me. She thought it would not be fair to Elise. I knew if you knew you would be careful——" but Judy could not let Molly finish.

"Careful! Elise jealous of me! Uncle Tom and me! Oh, Molly, Molly, how absurd! Why, Mr. Kinsella has kept close to me to be ready to catch Pierce by the heels and pull him out, in case I should decide to gobble him up. I thought everybody knew that. The only reason he decided to go off on this trip was that I had a heart-to-heart talk with him and told him that he need not have any fear of me, that I was—was—but never mind what I told him. Anyhow, he is not afraid I'll make a meal of his beloved Pierce."

"How about Pierce?" asked Molly. "Is he, too, relieved at his assured safety?"

"That kid!" sniffed Judy. "He is not in the least in love with anything but his art. I fancy it would bore him to death if he thought Uncle Tom and I had had that talk. He likes me just as he would another boy."

Molly felt very happy that the clouds were all clearing away and her friends were behaving as friends should. She went off to her lecture hoping that Mr. Kinsella and Elise would quickly come to an understanding, and glad that she and her beloved Judy were once more on the old confidential terms.

Mr. Kinsella and Elise did come to an understanding and that understanding was perfectly satisfactory to both of them. They spent a wonderful day together, following the trail Judy had taken the day before, the morning at St. Cloud, with luncheon later on at Versailles. But they did not dance with the wedding parties they met, nor did they take the wrong train and go to Chartres instead of back to Paris.

It seemed so marvelous to Mr. Kinsella that this young, handsome, brilliant girl should find anything in him to care for, middle-aged, careworn man that he felt himself to be. On the other hand, Elise was equally astonished that a man of Mr. Kinsella's keen intelligence and experience could put up with a foolish, silly girl like herself. He endeavored to make her understand what a remarkable young woman she really was; and she tried equally hard to explain to him that his age was one of his chief attractions in her eyes, but that his virtues were so numerous it was hard to tell which ones made her love him so much.

At any rate, they came back to Paris with a much better opinion of themselves than they had taken away. Mr. Kinsella looked more than ever like a gray-haired Pierce. He said he had taken a dip in the fountain of eternal youth and never intended to get a day older than he was. Elise's eyes were sparkling and her cheeks all aglow. Her mother could not have complained that she lacked animation now or that her sallow complexion needed steaming.

When they returned to the studio in Rue Brea, they found Mrs. Brown, Molly and Judy trying not to look expectant, but, as Judy said, "ready to pop with curiosity." Elise ran to Mrs. Brown, and throwing her arms around her dear chaperone, hid her blushing face on her shoulder; while Mr. Kinsella, with boyish ingenuousness, said: "Well, what do you think? Elise and I have gone and done it!"

Enthusiastic congratulations followed and no one asked the question: "Done what?"

"We thought at first we would not tell for a few days, but keep our secret; but I have been persuading Elise that there is no use in waiting for wedding finery. She is beautiful enough in the clothes she has. And we have determined to go to Rome, where Mrs. Huntington now is, and be married immediately."

"That will be splendid," declared Mrs. Brown, "but we are sorry not to have it here, so we can all be present. I hate to give up my girl, but, of course, she must go straight to her mother."

"The only thing I don't like about it is for me, of all people, to be the one to interrupt Elise's studies at the art school, after all my talk about its being so important for her to get in a winter of hard, continuous work! I am afraid Mrs. Huntington will think I am not very consistent," laughed the happy fiancé.

Molly was wondering, too, what Mrs. Huntington would think of the match. She hoped Mr. Kinsella had told Elise of his former attachment to her mother, and that Elise would be prepared for the more than probable taunts from that far from considerate lady. Mr. Kinsella was well aware of the disposition of his prospective mother-in-law, and had prepared Elise by divulging to her the fact that he had at one time been engaged to her mother; but he spared her the knowledge of her perfidy. Mrs. Huntington had already told her daughter of what she designated a conquest of Tom Kinsella, as she was ever inclined to boast of the number of scalps of former suitors and to wear them as ornaments.

Mrs. Huntington proved to be very much pleased with the alliance. She had tried to inform herself of Mr. Kinsella's affairs and had been delighted to learn that he was really rich. She was too keen an observer not to know that Mr. Kinsella's interest in Elise was not altogether because of her father, nor yet her artistic talent. She had predicted to herself from the first that Tom Kinsella was falling in love with her daughter, and felt that her wisest course was to take herself off and not interfere in any way.

Elise, accompanied by her adoring lover and Pierce (Pierce rather dazed by the rapidity of the proceedings), and chaperoned by a lady produced by the ever resourceful Marquis d'Ochtè, made her journey to Rome. She found her mother in a most gracious humor and not even inclined to object to the marriage being hurried. Elise had rather feared she would obstruct their plans with a plea for wedding clothes, but her mother knew very well when it was wise to acquiesce. She gave in very gracefully and actually consented to Elise's being married in a dress that was not absolutely new nor of the latest cut.

She felt repaid for her amiability when Mr. Kinsella informed her that his wife intended, with his entire approval, to make over the bulk of her fortune to her mother on her twenty-fifth birthday.

"I have enough for all of us, but I know you will be happier if you have an independent fortune," said the happy bridegroom. "I am so grateful to you for letting me have Elise that I wish I could do something to show my appreciation."

"All I can say is that Elise is a very fortunate girl," said Mrs. Huntington; and there was a glitter in her eye that looked hard but it was really an unaccustomed tear trying to form itself.

And so Elise and Mr. Kinsella went off on their honeymoon. We will not even try to find out where they went, but be glad to know that they found each other more and more delightful and congenial as time passed. Mr. Kinsella gave the impression more than ever of being a prematurely gray young man as happiness smoothed out the few lines in his face. Elise lost altogether the hard, bitter expression that had occasionally marred her beauty, and quickly blossomed into the sweet, lovely woman that Mother Nature had planned her to be but that her own mother had blindly and selfishly tried to nip in the bud.

CHAPTER XVI.

APPLE BLOSSOM TIME IN NORMANDY.

After the excitement occasioned by Elise's and Mr. Kinsella's sudden decision to go to Rome and be married, our friends in the Rue Brea settled down to weeks of hard work, interspersed with many delightful jaunts to theaters, picture galleries and places of interest in and near Paris.

Molly got much from the lectures at the Sorbonne and to her delight found she could "think in French." They say that is the true test of whether you know a language.

Judy and Pierce worked diligently at their respective art schools and made great progress. Judy took no more trips to the country alone. She said she was big enough, old enough, and ugly enough to take care of herself, but she was afraid she did not have sense enough.

Mrs. Brown was enjoying herself quite as much as the young people. Her cousin, the marchioness, looked to it that she did not become lonesome, including her in all of her plans, taking her shopping, to clubs and lectures, to teas and receptions. The Marquis d'Ochtè and his son Philippe were always delighted when the American cousins were able to dine with them, and they had many charming evenings in their company.

Philippe was a faithful courier, holding himself in readiness to conduct them any and everywhere. He confided to his mother that he could not decide which girl, Molly or Judy, he loved most.

"How happy could I be with either, were t'other dear charmer away," he sighed.

"Well, my opinion is you will fall between two stools if you can't decide which one you want," answered his mother a little sharply, considering that it was her beloved son she was addressing. "Of course Molly is my choice, but Judy is charming and lovely, and if you think you will be happier with her you must not consider me.

For my part, I have my doubts about either one of them accepting you." But Sally Bolling d'Ochtè was not quite her honest self when she made that last remark, as she did not see how any girl in her senses could refuse her beautiful young son. "Next week we will all be at *Roche Craie* and maybe you can fix your seesawing heart. Cousin Mildred and the girls are delighted at the thought of getting out to the country for awhile, and goodness knows, I'll be glad to quit the glitter of Paris for a quiet rest."

All of them were glad to have a change. The spring was well under way. Paris was never more beautiful, with flowers everywhere; but Mrs. Brown confessed to being a little tired of housekeeping; and Molly was looking a little fagged. The lecture rooms were hot and the dinners at the restaurants were not so delightful, now that the novelty had worn off. Spring fever was the real matter with them and a good lazy time at the chateau in Normandy was all that was necessary to put them on their feet again. Pierce Kinsella had been included in the invitation, as the marchioness slyly told her son, to take care of the girl that he, Philippe, would finally decide not to be the one of all others for him.

Roche Craie was very interesting to the Americans. It was a castle literally dug out of chalk cliffs. The so-called new chateau (only about two hundred years old), was built out in front, but the original old castle was little more than a cave or series of caves. The family used only the new part but kept it all in absolute repair. The architecture was pure Gothic, vaulted roofs and pointed arches. Where the roof and walls were dug in the chalk, there was an attempt at carving, carrying out the Gothic spirit. Huge chimneys had their openings in the fields overhead, and strange, indeed, did it seem to find one of these old chimneys in a wheat field with poppies and corn flowers growing in its crevices.

"A very convenient country for Santa Claus to ply his trade," said Molly to Philippe, who was showing her over the estate. "But what is this peaked thing with the cross on it?"

"Oh, that is the steeple to the chapel, which is dug very far back under the hill and is one of the most interesting things about *Roche Craie*. We did not take you there this morning when we were showing you over the old castle, as my mother has a kind of horror of it and hates to go in it. There is a ghost story connected with it, and you must know by this time how *ma mère* shuns the disagreeable things of this life," answered Philippe, looking at Molly with growing admiration. Some persons seem to belong out of doors and Molly was one of them. Her clear, fine complexion could stand the searchlight of the brightest sun, her hair was like burnished gold, her eyes, Philippe thought, like the bluets in the fields of Normandy.

"Cousin Molly, you remind me of the beautiful Jehane de Saint-Pol. Jehane of the Fair Girdle, the beloved of Richard C[oe]ur de Lion, Richard Yea-and-Nay. Her eyes were gray green while yours are of the most wonderful blue, but there is something about your height and slenderness, your poise, the set of your head, the glory of your hair that suggests her. If Mother gives the fancy dress ball that she is threatening, please go as Jehane. I should like to go as Richard."

Molly blushed. She was always confused by compliments and personalities and hoped Philippe would stop pressing them on her. They had been pleasant companions in Paris and she had liked being with him very much. He was extremely agreeable and well-informed, handsome and charming, but Molly preferred him as a cousin to a courtier. She had an idea that the title of "Yea-and-Nay" was rather suitable for him, more suitable than "Lion Hearted."

"Please tell me the ghost story about the chapel," she begged, changing the subject adroitly.

"All right, if you won't tell mother I told it. She has a horror of it and is afraid the servants might get timid and refuse to stay here alone while we are in Paris, if the old tale were revived. My people, you perhaps know, were Huguenots. The archives show that it was from flocks of sheep belonging to *Roche Craie* that the wool was taken to send as a present to Queen Elizabeth of England, in return for her gift of nine pieces of cannon to the downtrodden Huguenots.

"The owner of *Roche Craie* was one Jean d'Ochtè, a man of great intelligence and integrity. He had been a gay courtier at the court of Charles IX, but, there, had come under the influence of Admiral Coligny and had turned Huguenot. His wife, much younger than himself, the beautiful Elizabeth, a cousin of the Guises, followed her husband's example but saw no reason why she need give up all gaiety and pleasure because of her change of heart. But Jean took her away from the court and all of its dissipations and dangers and brought her here to the old chateau, where she was literally buried alive in stupidity and ennui.

"Jean fought with the Prince of Condé against the Guises, but when peace was finally declared in 1570, I think it was, he came back to *Roche Craie* and began to get his estate in order. Elizabeth besought him to take her back to court where she had been a great favorite, but he feared that the life of gaiety would undermine her not too strenuous piety, and refused.

"The Huguenots were seemingly in great favor with Catherine de Medicis, who was preparing for her great coup, the Massacre of St. Bartholomew. The d'Ochtès were not overlooked by the cruel queen, but a guard was sent to *Roche Craie* headed by a zealous Jesuit. Jean was murdered in his bed but Elizabeth escaped with her little son Henri to the chapel. She shut the great iron door and managed to place the heavy bar so that the soldiers could not open it, but the artful Jesuit came up into this field and made the soldiers tear down the steeple and then he lowered himself into the chapel with a rope. It was raining in torrents and as the steeple was removed the floor was deluged. Elizabeth hid her little son behind the altar and ran to the door hoping, it is supposed, to divert the attention of the furious priest from her son to herself. She shrieked, and the soldiers in the field above heard her agonizing cry, 'God help me, God help me!'

"There was a tremendous clap of thunder and a blinding flash of lightning. The Jesuit lunged forward with his dagger raised, but the lightning struck before he could, and he and the Lady Elizabeth met death at the same moment. Strange to say, the little Henri, hiding behind the altar, was unharmed. The bolt from heaven had come straight through the aperture made by tearing down this steeple, not touching the soldiers in the field above or the frightened child below. It is said that the bodies of the lady and the priest were both entirely consumed. The soldiers, taking it as a sign from heaven, spared the young heir of *Roche Craie*; otherwise, the race would have been exterminated on that dreadful day.

"And now for the ghost story after my long narrative, which I am afraid must have bored you sadly."

"Oh, don't think it! I have been thrilled by it. Please go on," exclaimed Molly.

"You are very kind to find it interesting. It always excites me, especially when I think how close little Henri was to being killed; and had he not been spared, I myself could never have come into existence."

"That would have been a calamity, indeed," laughed Molly.

"Would it have made any difference to you, Cousin Molly? I should like to think it would have made some difference to you," and Philippe looked rather more ardent than Molly liked to see him.

"Of course it would make loads of difference to all of us, Philippe. But the ghost story, the ghost story! I believe you are afraid to tell it to me."

"Well, the legend runs that on a stormy night if the floor of the chapel, which is paved with soapstone, gets wet, the footprints of the Lady Elizabeth, where she ran across the deluged floor, are plainly visible. She was just out of her bed and her feet were bare. They say it shows she had a very small foot with a high arch, the print of the heel, a space where the instep arches over, and then the ball of the foot and the tiny toes. Peasants passing in the field above have heard (provided the night is stormy enough), the agonizing cry, 'God help me, God help me!' seeming to come from the old steeple."

"How wonderful! But tell me, have you never seen the footprints yourself?"

"Mother has such a horror of the story and the talk about ghosts that I have spared her feelings and never put the legend to the test. I used to think I'd go some stormy night alone to the chapel, but when the stormy nights come I am too sleepy or too indolent or afraid of disturbing mother or something else turns up, and I never have done it."

The young heir of the d'Ochtès led his cousin to a higher point of the hill overlooking the chateau where he could show her the whole estate of *Roche Craie*. It was a beautiful sight. The gentle hills sloped to the Seine with here and there a sharp cleft showing a cliff of chalk, standing out very white against the green of the spring grass.

Some of the peasants had their homes in the cliffs, and Philippe assured Molly that they were very comfortable, dry houses. It was a vast estate in the highest state of cultivation. The village was clean and prosperous, consisting of about twenty houses besides the ones dug in the cliffs, two shops and an inn. Across the river was a forest of great trees that made the beeches at Chatsworth seem saplings.

"Is the land across the river yours, too?" she asked.

"Yes, indeed, that is the best part of *Roche Craie*. My studies at Nancy have taught me what to do to keep our forest, and I am at work now preserving those beautiful old trees. You do like it here, don't you, Cousin Molly? It does not seem small and mean to you after Chatsworth, does it?"

"Small and mean! It is beautiful, the most beautiful place I ever saw! You must not get an idea that Chatsworth is magnificent like this."

As Molly looked out across the hills of this splendid French estate she thought of her home in Kentucky, of the beech woods and the orchard as it was before the old tree they called their castle blew down; and then she began to wonder what the orchard looked like now with Professor Green's bungalow occupying the site of the old castle. There had been no letter for her from Wellington, the week before she left Paris for Normandy, and the girl had secretly hoped it meant perhaps that her friend was on the eve of his departure from America. She longed for some definite news both of Professor Green and her brother Kent.

"What are you thinking about, Cousin Molly?"

"Apple trees," answered Molly, coming back to earth.

"Oh, are you especially fond of apple trees? I must show you the orchard over this hill. It is in bloom and a very beautiful sight. Not much to look at unless it is in bloom, however," and Philippe conducted Molly over the brow of another hill where a very orderly apple orchard was in full bloom.

Philippe broke off a spray for her. "I must not let the steward see me do such a thing. The old man would count the blossoms and tell me I had spoiled so many apples."

Molly buried her face in the cluster of flowers and her thoughts flew back again to the trees at Chatsworth, not the orderly, trimmed ones like these of Normandy, but old and gnarled and twisted. The dream she had had on the steamer came back to her and again she felt Edwin Green leaning over her, looking at her with his kind brown eyes and saying: "Molly, this is *your* orchard home."

She was awakened from her revery by Philippe, who seized her hand, apple blossoms and all, and addressed her in the most impassioned tones: "Cousin Molly! Molly, dearest Molly! I have longed for this moment as I want to tell you how much I am gratified that you like *Roche Craie*. The place means so much to my mother and father and to me that we are happy when any one likes it, but for you of all persons to be pleased with it, adds to its value in our eyes. We all of us want you to make your home here. I know it would be more convenable for me to address your mother first, but since I am half American you will pardon me if I let that half speak to you, and later on the French half can arrange with your charming mother."

Molly was greatly mystified. At first she had feared that Philippe was going to make love to her when he had seized her hand with so much ardor; but it turned out that he was merely offering *Roche Craie* as a home to her mother and herself in the name of the Marquis and Marquise d'Ochtè. She was greatly relieved that he was not going to be sentimental and answered him gratefully:

"You are very kind, Philippe, but mother and I have our home in Kentucky, and while we are enjoying our stay in France, every moment of it, we have every intention of returning to our own country in the course of time. I cannot answer for mother, but I am almost sure she will take the same stand I do."

"But should she not, would you abide by her decision, like a dutiful daughter?" exclaimed Philippe eagerly. "My own mother has been very happy in her adopted country and you are strangely like her in some ways."

"Yes, but Cousin Sally had every reason for remaining in France. She had her Jean——"

"Ah," interrupted Philippe, "would not you have your Philippe? Could I not be as much to you as my father has been to my mother?"

At last Molly understood. Her cousin was proposing to her. Molly was by nature so kind that her first feeling was one of pity for the young man as she hated to hurt his feelings; but she was sure that he did not love her in the least and that her refusal of him would astonish him but not give him a single heartache.

"Philippe," she answered, looking him straight in the eye without sign of coquetry or softness, "you know very well you could never be to me what your father is to your mother; and one of the biggest reasons is that I am not to you what your mother is to your father and never could be. You are not in love with me nor am I in love with you. I have liked you a whole lot and I believe you like me, but there must be more than mere liking to make it right to marry. I don't see how you could have lived always in the house with your mother and father, who are as much sweethearts now as when they first married, and not understand something about real love."

Philippe's feelings ran the gamut from astonishment and embarrassment to humility. He was not by nature a conceited fellow, but so many mothers and fathers of so many demoiselles had approached him with a view to an alliance for those daughters, that it had never really entered his head that, when the time came for him to make a decision in choice of a wife, he would be refused. He did like Molly very much, liked and admired her, found her agreeable and interesting, lovely to behold and such a lady, and at the same time so perfectly acceptable to his beloved mother and father. She was in fact so entirely suitable to become the future Marquise d'Ochtè. Had his mother not made a wonderful success as a marchioness? Were she and Molly not of the same blood and traditions? True, he did not have for Molly the grand passion that novelists write of; but a sincere liking might last longer than the so-called grand passion.

Molly's words brought him upstanding. After all, he did not understand anything about real love, not as much as this chit of an American girl. He bowed his head for a moment in deep dejection, and then, shrugging his shoulders, he smiled into her stern eyes a little wistfully.

"I thank you, Cousin Molly, for your salutary admonishment. You are right; I do not know what real love means. I have an idea I could learn, though, with as good a teacher as I am sure you would be. I value your friendship and liking so much that I am going to ask you to forget that I have made this stupid proposal and let us continue the good comrades we have been."

"Oh, Philippe, I have already forgotten it! You must not think I was severe, but I do like you so much I hated for you to demean yourself."

"There is one thing I should like to ask you, Cousin Molly: how do you happen to know so much about true love?" And the young man, his equanimity entirely restored, looked teasingly at his cousin. "Is it entirely theoretical?"

CHAPTER XVII.

THE GHOST IN THE CHAPEL.

Philippe told his mother of the outcome of his proposal to Molly and when he repeated her remark about her and her Jean, the good lady shed tears of remorse that she had encouraged Philippe to want to marry a girl that she well knew her son did not really and truly love. Molly's answer made her realize even more than before the fine, true heart of her little Kentucky cousin, and her regret was very great that Molly was not to become the bride of her son.

"Ah, my boy, how stupid we have been! Here you and I have gone serenely on all winter, confident that either one of these lovely girls, Judy or Molly, was ready to drop like a ripe plum if you but touched the tree. We never once thought of the damage we might do one of the girls. Suppose you had engaged the affections of both of them, while you were deciding which one you wanted the more? Thank goodness, there are no hearts broken, not even yours. Tell me, dear: will you try for Judy now?"

"As our American friends say: 'Not on your life,'" laughed Philippe. "Molly has taught me a lesson. I am not in love with Miss Julia Kean even as much as with my cousin, and with the example of happiness ever before my eyes that you and my father present, I shall be very careful and pick out for my wife one whom I truly love and who, I hope, truly loves me. I can't quite see how I escaped falling deeply in love with Cousin Molly. She is so sweet and so everything that I admire. Do you know, *ma mère*, I have an idea that the Providence that looks after children and fools has protected me from a calamity which falling in love with Molly would have been? I have a feeling that my little cousin is already in love with someone else, and that there never has been a chance for me."

"Well, what a wise young man a refusal has made of you!" teased his mother. "Two or three more experiences of the sort will make a real savant of you. What makes you have this feeling, this pricking in your thumbs?"

"Something about the way she spoke of love. Her eyes are certainly the mirrors of her soul, and there was a look in them that made me feel she knew what she was talking about."

"Well, we never can tell. I am glad my thoughtlessness and stupidity have not done any damage," said the marchioness, looking fondly at her handsome son and thinking in her heart that both girls must be either blind or already very much in love not to be crazy about her Adonis.

That night, the soft white clouds that had been the despair of Judy and Pierce all day as they had vainly tried to put them on canvas, came together and managed to make a very large black cloud which finally filled the whole heavens; and a fierce thunder storm ensued.

Molly and Judy lay awake talking. Judy had the hardihood to accuse Molly of having turned down a chance to become the future Marquise d'Ochtè.

"How on earth do you know, Judy? I would never think of telling such a thing even to you, my very best friend. It seems a very unfair advantage to take of a man, to let people know he has been refused. But you are the greatest guesser in the world."

"It didn't take much guessing to come to this conclusion. Who's a mole now, you old bat? I have known for some time that the handsome Philippe has had us both under consideration and it was a toss up which one would be honored. I was betting on you but hoping I would draw the prize," laughed Judy.

"Oh, Judy!" exclaimed Molly, shocked a little and wondering if, after all, Judy was just flirting with her brother Kent.

"Oh, I didn't want to accept him, but I just wanted to jar him a little! I like him very much and am crazy about his mother and father, but his complacency in regard to you and me has rather—rather—well, 'got my goat.' I don't know how else to put it. It has never entered his aristocratic French mind that we would think of refusing him. He isn't exactly conceited, in fact, I don't think he is at all conceited; but things have come his way too much all his life.

"But my, wouldn't it be great to be mistress of this wonderful place? The chateau is simply perfect and the country around just screaming to be painted. Pierce and I found so many motifs this morning that I know I could live here a hundred years and not paint half of them. I am afraid if Philippe had chosen 'Apple Blossom Time in Normandy' to make love to me; and had first taken me on a high hill and shown me all of his wonderful estates, that I should have been tempted to make a *marriage de convenance*, in spite of my desire to jar your handsome cousin. Pierce and I were on the opposite hill trying to paint some cloud effects when Philippe broke off a spray of apple blossoms and gave it to you. I couldn't help seeing what ensued; but I got in front of Pierce, so he missed the tableau; and he was so taken up with the clouds that he did not know he was missing anything."

Molly was thankful for the darkness that hid her hot face. But the storm was becoming so severe that Judy dropped the subject and got up to look out of the window for more cloud effects.

"Oh, Judy, I forgot to tell you that Philippe told me the ghost story connected with the old chateau! Come on back to bed and I'll tell it to you," said Molly.

Judy accordingly abandoned the study of the storm clouds and eagerly drank in every word Molly had to tell her of the beautiful Elizabeth and the terrible night of Saint Bartholomew.

"Oh, Molly, delicious thrills are running up and down my backbone? And you say Philippe has never been to the chapel on a stormy night to test the truth of the story? Lived here all his life and never had the get-up-and-get to go find out? That is the keynote of his character. He lacks imagination, and that is one big reason both of us have had for not succumbing to his charms. There is no telling what havoc he might have played with our hearts if he had had more imagination."

Then both girls lay still listening to the storm, each one thinking of another good reason she had for not falling in love with poor Philippe, even if he had been gifted with the imagination of a Byron.

"Oh, what a clap of thunder!" Judy clutched Molly and held her close. "I have always been more afraid of thunder than lightning.

Molly, I wonder if Elizabeth's footprints wouldn't be visible on such a night? Let's go see. I can't sleep for thinking of her. We can easily get there without being seen or heard."

Wrapped in their kimonos and armed with Judy's electric searchlight and a big pitcher of water, as Philippe had said the floor must be wet to bring out the footprints, the girls made their way to the haunted chapel. They groped along narrow passages connecting the new chateau with the old. There was an entrance to the chapel through the old chateau made since the fatal night of Saint Bartholomew, but the girls were not aware of it. They opened a narrow door on the court and ran through the pouring rain to the great door of the chapel. It was not locked but very heavy and it took their combined strength to push it open. The few moments that it took to accomplish this were enough for them to become wet to the skin.

How dark and grewsome the chapel was! The storm was raging. Looking up through the cracks in the little steeple, they could see flash after flash of continuous white lightning. They might have spared themselves the trouble of bringing the pitcher of water as the floor was already very wet from the leaks in the steeple. Molly clutched Judy, trying to keep from screaming, as something brushed her cheek.

"Something touched me! There it is again!" But the searchlight proved it to be nothing more than a great thick rope hanging from the steeple.

"Could it be the one the Jesuit came down?" gasped Judy.

"Hardly," whispered Molly. "Ropes don't last four hundred years. It must be the bell rope."

"Of course," exclaimed Judy, reassured. "What a stupid I am! But come on, we must examine the floor. Let's see: she started at the altar where she had concealed the boy, and then ran towards the door. The footprints should be along here where we are standing. Not enough wetness here." Judy turned over the pitcher and Molly had to jump to keep her feet out of the water. The girls stooped and began examining every inch of the flagging.

"Judy, Judy, look!" cried Molly. "This is a footprint. It stays dry while all the floor is wet. Look, the little toes and then a space for the high arch and then the slender little heel! Here is another and another."

Tense with excitement the girls stood up and faced each other. There was an extra loud crash of thunder and a vivid flash of lightning. There emerged from behind the altar a tall figure in a priest's black cowl, carrying a lantern.

If there had been any peasants in the field passing the old steeple on this night of terrible storm, they would have been able to bear witness to the truth of the ghost story of the beautiful Elizabeth. There was certainly a shriek of "God help me! God help me!" but it came from the over-wrought Judy. Molly reasoned quickly that ghosts of Jesuits would not carry kerosene lanterns; and, besides, that ghosts do not as a rule appear to two persons at the same time.

The man put down his lantern on the altar and threw back his hood, disclosing the features of Philippe. His lantern had little effect on the blackness of the chapel and Molly had turned off their searchlight at sight of the apparition. Philippe peered into the darkness and spoke with a slight agitation:

"Is some one in the chapel? I thought I heard a scream, but the thunder was so loud I am not sure."

Judy sat down in the puddle made by the overturned pitcher and gave a dry sob, while Molly turned on the searchlight and called out:

"Nobody but two penitents, Brother Philippe."

"Well, you gave me quite a turn! I thought you were at least the poor murdered Elizabeth," and Philippe strode forward and assisted the trembling Judy to her feet. "I couldn't sleep and I thought I would come and test the truth of the old tale about the footprints. I felt somehow that I had lacked in imagination never to have done it before. Certainly you girls have no lack of it."

"I wish I did lack a little of the abundance I possess," shuddered Judy. "I was as certain a moment ago that you were the murderous Jesuit as I am now that you are Philippe d'Ochtè. But tell me: how did you get behind the altar without our seeing you; and where did you get that cloak? It is about the most picturesque thing I ever saw."

"There is an entrance to the old chateau from behind the altar; and as for my cloak it is an ordinary *gens d'arme* cape. It does look rather monkish. If you admire it, I will present it to you. It will make good studio property."

The young people had to examine the footprints more carefully, and of course Philippe discovered that they were really raised places in the rock, and for that reason showed when the floor was wet.

He conducted the girls back to the main building through the narrow corridor that had entrance to the chapel through a small door behind the altar.

"If you only had known of this way, you would have been spared a wetting. Both of you are drenched. There is a fire in the library. If you will come there you can dry off. I am so afraid you will catch cold," said Philippe. "I think you girls are a spunky pair. I have never known a French girl who would have dared to go on the adventure you have to-night."

"Well, I fancy we would not have dared to go had we really believed in ghosts. As for drying ourselves by the library fire I think we had much better go off to bed. We might rouse the household. Cousin Sally is not to know of our escapade, as you say she has a dread of this old story getting started up again," said Molly.

The two bade their young host good-night and crept quietly to their room.

"My, don't dry clothes and warm covers feel good!" exclaimed Judy, snuggling down in the lavender-scented linen sheets. "Molly, I was never more frightened in my life than when that figure appeared behind the altar! My not really believing in ghosts did not help me one bit. Did you ever see anything in the way of a mere man quite so excruciatingly handsome as Philippe when he threw back his cowl and stood bareheaded peering into the darkness?"

"Oh, Judy, what a girl you are! How could you take note of all that when you were in a little heap on the floor sobbing out your soul?"

"I peeped through my fingers. People don't sob with their eyes. What a picture he would make!" and Judy began to draw in the air. "Golden hair and beard, with the black peaked hood half off and that expression of looking into the future that he had when he spoke to ask who was there! 'The Young Prophet,' must be the title. He seems to have a latent imagination, after all. I believe I have done him an injustice. An awful pity one of us can't marry him! Somehow we ought to keep him in the family. I bet you I know why your Cousin Sally hates to have the ghost talked about! I just know she has made a trip to the chapel in a spirit of adventure and got good and scared."

But Molly was breathing so quietly that Judy realized she was talking to the air, making no more impression than her imaginary brush had made when she painted the wonderful picture of "The Young Prophet."

CHAPTER XVIII.

THE PRESCRIPTION.

Paris was as pleasant to return to as it had been to leave. The change and rest in the country had put new life in all of the marchioness's guests, and they were ready to go back to their duties with renewed interest and vigor.

They found on their arrival, however, interruptions to their work more potent than plain spring fever:—Professor Edwin Green and Kent Brown had reached Paris the day before, intending to surprise their friends, and had been themselves both surprised and disappointed to find the apartment in Rue Brea closed. Miss Josephine Williams had come to the fore with information and kindly offers of tea and *brioche*. Professor Green was thrown into the depths of despair when he learned that the absent ones were visiting the d'Ochtès in Normandy, and Kent could not conceal his misery when Jo let out that Pierce Kinsella was one of the party.

That young woman, with a feminine instinct that belied her masculine attire, understood the two men, and divining that they were both in love and jealous, one of Philippe and the other of Pierce, exercised the greatest tact and succeeded in sending them off to their hotel in a much better frame of mind. She did a great deal of quiet talking about how boyish Pierce Kinsella was, and what a pet to the whole community, being years younger than any of the girls. As for Philippe she touched lightly on his evident admiration for Elise O'Brien before her marriage and hinted that he seemed equally pleased with Frances Andrews now that Elise was off the carpet.

As the young men walked toward their student hotel on the Boulevarde Mont Parnesse, they agreed that Jo Bill was a pretty nice sort. They had been so impressed by the quality of her tea and *brioche* and her kindly tact in telling them exactly what they wanted to hear about their lady loves and their feared rivals, that they had forgotten to notice her trousers and her tousled red hair and spoke only of her honest mouth and good teeth, friendly eyes and shapely feet.

Professor Green had been threatened with a nervous breakdown and President Walker had at the eleventh hour been able to procure a substitute. The wise President understood very well that there was a cure to his nervous breakdown, but that it had to be taken on the other side of the Atlantic; so she was delighted to hasten his departure. Edwin had telegraphed Kent of his intended sailing, and that young man had joyously made preparations to join him in New York. He had the great pleasure of paying a visit of condolence to his Aunt Sarah Clay, who had at last lost her suit against the Oil Trust. He also had the pleasure of depositing in the safety vault a goodly number of bonds for his beloved mother, enough to insure a comfortable income to her and the certainty that her financial worries were over forever.

"This is what I call an anticlimax," said Edwin to Kent the next morning as they lounged on the Pont Carrousel. "We got ourselves ready for the excitement of surprising the ladies yesterday and nothing came off, and now this hanging around waiting has taken all the life out of me. Miss Williams insisted we could not miss them if we guarded the Pont Carrousel, and of course this would be the natural way for them to come from the Gare du Nord; but things don't seem to be happening in the natural way here, lately."

Kent looked narrowly at his friend. He did look tired and depressed, but the voyage had done him good. He was better than he had been at Wellington when Dr. McLean had given him a thorough going over and, after a consultation with his wise partner (Mrs. McLean), had prescribed an immediate sea trip as the only cure for his malady.

"Oh, buck up, old man, the worst is yet to come!" Kent gave him an affectionate push just as a taxicab came lumbering on the far end of the bridge and he saw a blue scarf floating in the breezes, a blue scarf that could belong to no one but his dear sister Molly. "What did I tell you? There they are now. Now get ready for the anticlimax that you so scorn. I bet it will out-climax the climax!"

Judy was the first to see the young men. "Stop, stop!" she called to the chauffeur.

"Extra charge if I stop, Mademoiselle," warned the man, slowing down his car.

"Oh, these Frenchies!" wailed the excited girl. "They part mother and son for three sous; and — and — —" but she did not finish about whom else they would part.

Edwin and Kent crowded in on the front seat with the greedy chauffeur, and the happy crowd was quickly taken to the Rue Brea.

As Professor Green gazed over his shoulder into the sweet eyes of Molly Brown, he knew that the sea trip was just exactly what he needed to restore his failing health and that his old friend Dr. McLean was a wise physician.

Molly, on the back seat with her mother and Judy, felt very happy. Had she not cause to feel so? Was not her beloved brother on the seat in front of her after being parted from them for months and months? Was not her mother's face a picture of maternal joy to be once again near her boy? Did not her dear friend Julia Kean frankly show her delight at Kent's proximity? And last, and Molly tried to make herself think it the least reason, was not her friend Professor Green rattling along in the taxi with them with an expression in his kind eyes as they gazed into hers that made her drop her own, fearing that hers might have the same telltale look to him that his had to her?

Kent overpaid the chauffeur in spite of Judy's protestations and then Professor Green came back and gave him an extra *pourboire*.

"Let us squander our hard-earned wealth if we want to, Miss Judy," begged Kent. "When I saw that man's round, red face looming up in front of Molly and mother and you, it seemed to me that he looked like a veritable cupid; and I should like to give him a good big tip just for bringing us all together again."

"All right, but Fate ought to be tipped instead of that red-faced, avaricious old Frenchy," laughed Judy.

What a talk they did have when they got themselves settled comfortably in the studio, which the kindly Jo Williams and Polly Perkins had aired and freshened up for their arrival!

Kent had to tell all the Kentucky news first, as Mrs. Brown and Molly were eager to hear every detail concerning the loved ones at home. The report was a good one: John and Paul were doing well in their chosen professions; Sue was happy as a lark with her Cyrus, who was having the "muddy lane" macadamized; a recent letter from Ernest said that he would take his holiday in August, provided his mother and Molly would have returned to Kentucky by that time; Aunt Clay was in a pleasant, chastened mood, seeming rather reconciled to losing her suit; Aunt Mary, the dear old cook, was lonesome and forlorn with "Ole Miss and Molly Baby done gone so fer away. Looks lak I ain't got the heart to put a livin' thing inter a pie sence they done gone an' lef' me. I cyarn't eat fer a thinkin' what kind er messes they is puttin' in they own innerds; an I cyarn't sleep fer thinkin' of the deep waters a rollin' betwixt us." Mrs. Brown and Molly had to wipe their eyes at Kent's description of the dear old darkey.

"Speaking of innerds," laughed Kent, "where are we to have luncheon? This constant change of climate is giving me a powerful good appetite. My only regret in regard to our crossing was that we did not come on a German line. The French line is good enough except that they have only four meals a day, while I am told the German has six."

"Oh, you greedy!" said Molly, giving him a little extra hug for luck. "How would you like to have a spread in the studio? Judy and I will gladly show you what we can do. I'll go forage right now."

"The very thing!" exclaimed Judy. "You attend to the meat and dessert, and I'll hold up the salad end. Now, Mrs. Brown, you must rest and not do one thing but entertain the gentlemen, while Molly and I hustle around."

"I think the gentlemen had much better go with you and Molly and help forage. I will lie down and take a real rest while all of you are gone," said Mrs. Brown with a whimsical smile.

As they went out, Kent said to Judy: "What a brick Mumsy is, anyhow!" Edwin Green said nothing, but he thought: "Mrs. Brown's tact and kindness are never failing."

He was eager to see Molly alone, but when they were alone he found he had not the courage to say to her the words that were in his heart. They talked of Wellington and their mutual friends. He had news to tell of Richard Blount and Melissa Hathaway which gave Molly great delight.

"The mountain would not go to Mohammed, so Mohammed is going to the mountain. There is an excellent opening for Richard in a Kentucky mountain town, Pineville, as a railroad lawyer, and he has accepted. Melissa has been appointed supervisor of the schools for the district, and Miss Allfriend assures Melissa she can do more good to her beloved mountains in this way than by merely teaching, so she has accepted. Miss Allfriend is very happy at this outcome. She has seen her own youth go in the uphill work and is so glad to know that Melissa is to have a life of her own. Melissa and Richard are to be married in June."

"How splendid!" exclaimed Molly, clasping her hands and thinking what a silly girl she had been to fancy that Professor Green might care for the beautiful mountain girl otherwise than as a friend. "I know they will be very happy, and I believe Melissa will not let matrimony interfere with what she considers her life work."

"Dicky Blount declares he will never be jealous of such small things as mountains. That is rather complimentary to me, as he did me the honor to be jealous of me," laughed the professor.

"Why, how ridiculous!" and Molly plunged into the poultry shop, where the blazing fire accounted to her companion for her heightened color. The proprietor had an extra pullet on the spit roasting for a chance customer. He pronounced it "*charmante et tendre*," and the hungry crowd declared he was right.

The luncheon was perfect. Everyone was happy and so much talk was the order of the day that Jo Williams poked her head in to see what the row was about, and they made her stay to dessert; and then Polly Perkins came to see where Jo was, and they invited him to stay to coffee.

"You have had a very successful winter, have you not?" said Edwin Green to Mrs. Brown, while Molly and Judy cleared the table and Kent went over to Polly's studio to see the portrait of Mrs. Pace.

"Yes, indeed, most delightful. I have been much disappointed in not having Kent with us, and now that he has come, I must soon leave him here and go back to all the others. They need me, especially old Aunt Mary. I could never forgive myself if anything should happen to the old woman while I am away. She is getting very feeble. I fancy Kent will do well enough without me. He makes friends so easily and then dear Judy is to be here for another year at least."

As Judy leaned over her to arrange the bowl of flowers on the table, Mrs. Brown smiled on her as though she were already her daughter.

CHAPTER XIX.

FONTAINEBLEAU AND WHAT CAME OF IT.

Molly's promise to wait to see the Forest of Fontainebleau with him had kept up Edwin Green's spirits through the long winter, and now he eagerly planned the excursion to that historic spot. They were to take the early morning train; spend the forenoon seeing the palace; have lunch at a restaurant that Edwin remembered of old; then walk or ride through the Forest as the ladies should decide; and spend the night at Barbizon.

Everything was coming up to his dreams. Even the day was perfect. He was allowed to sit by Molly on the train and later on to be by her side while the guide showed them through the palace and over the beautiful grounds. Mrs. Brown and Judy and Kent were inseparable.

"The poor old boy has been sick and my opinion is he needs a little Molly-coddling; so let's give him all the chance in the world," whispered Kent to Judy; and Judy fell in with the suggestion and hooked her arm in Mrs. Brown's with a "Whither thou goest, I will go" look.

They had luncheon at a restaurant, The Sign of the Swan, kept by an old English couple, who made a specialty of roast beef and English mustard.

"None of the ready mixed French stuff that is so mild you can eat it by itself, but the good English brand that will really burn," said the buxom madame, as she smilingly served great slabs of rare beef with generous helpings of freshly mixed mustard.

"It burns all right, all right," exclaimed Kent between gulps of water. "It would be invaluable for outside application, but I advise all of you to go easy on how you place it in the interior. The English have stopped wearing visible armor but my opinion is they have swallowed it to protect their insides from the onslaught of their own mustard."

"I think it is delicious," said Molly.

"So do I," echoed Edwin. "I never tasted better."

Kent gave the professor a quizzical glance and then flicked his eyelid at Judy. The young man was very far gone, he thought, if he could swallow that mustard and make out he enjoyed it, since he, Kent, happened to know that Edwin Green abhorred all highly seasoned food. But forsooth, if Molly liked mustard he would like mustard, too.

Molly and Judy had expressed their desire to walk through the Forest to Barbizon but Mrs. Brown was to take the diligence, as it was rather too long a walk for her to attempt. Judy suddenly decided that she was tired and would ride with Mrs. Brown, and Kent declared that he needed assistance to carry the quantity of roast beef he had consumed at The Sign of the Swan, and was delighted to be spared the walk of several miles.

"I tell you, I almost sang my 'Swan Song' when I got that first mouthful of mustard, and it would have been to the tune of 'It's a hot time in the old town to-night.' If you and the professor are going to walk, Molly, you had better start now and not wait for the diligence to be off."

So Molly and Edwin did start on the walk that the young man had been looking forward to for so many months. The Forest of Fontainebleau is a wonderful spot and a fitting place for a young man to use as the setting for his day dreams. Here he was actually doing the thing he had been dreaming of, only it was more delightful than he had let himself think it could be. Molly was all loveliness and sweetness. He blessed the miles that made it necessary for Mrs. Brown to ride; he blessed the unusual fatigue that had overtaken Judy; and above all, he blessed the slabs of rare roast beef that had put Kent out of the running. So blind was he to everything but Molly, the color of her eyes and hair, the curve of her cheek and sweetness of her mouth, that he had not seen that Kent and Judy had deliberately given up the walk for his sake. Julia Kean did not know what "tired" meant, and as for Kent, he was a young man of unlimited capacity.

They soon left the broad avenue and struck into one of the by-paths going in the direction of Barbizon. Edwin had a map of the Forest on which every path was indicated, and with the help of the many finger-posts, they were able to locate themselves from time to time.

"Is it as beautiful as you thought it would be, Miss Molly?"

"Oh, more beautiful! I never have seen such trees. It is so wonderful, too, to think that there are no snakes. They say they have not seen a snake in these parts for over fifty years. When I am in the woods, I am always a little bit uneasy about snakes."

"Since there are no snakes, we might sit down on this moss-covered rock and rest."

There was more to Edwin's dream than simply walking through the woods with Molly; and he felt that no more suitable place could be found than this sylvan spot where she could be seated like a queen on a throne while he poured out assurances of his life-long allegiance, if she would but admit him as a subject.

"Oh, Miss Molly! Molly, my darling, I am dumb with love of you. I want to tell you how much I love you; how long I have loved you. Can you love me just a little?"

And Molly raised her frank blue eyes to his appealing brown ones and answered: "No, I can't love you just a little, but I have to love you a whole lot."

His day dream was indeed coming true: alone with Molly Brown in the great, deep, silent forest, his love spoken at last and Molly actually confessing that she cared for him. That eminent instructor of English at Wellington College found when the time came to express himself that all his knowledge of words was as naught, and the only English he had at his command was: "I love you, do you love me?" and "I have loved you since the day in your Freshman year when you got locked in the corridor. How long have you loved me, if you do really love me?"

They finally resumed their walk, but now they went hand in hand. How much there was to talk about, how many things to explain!

"And will you be willing to spend the summers in your orchard home with me? I have always called it 'Molly's Orchard Home' in my mind."

"I can think of no place in the world where I'd rather spend the summers. Would I not be near all of my people? I am so glad you asked my advice about the bungalow! Now the doors open the way I want them to; and the cellar has an outside entrance; and the guest chamber has those extra inches on it, besides the nice big closet; and the attic steps are big enough to get a trunk up. Did you really and truly think it was going to be my home when you were planning it?"

"I could only hope and hope and plan and dream. For almost six years I have known that it was you or nobody for me. Ever since you came to Wellington, a slip of a girl, it has been all I could do to keep from claiming you. You were too young. I knew it would not be fair to try to tie you to an old dry-as-dust like me until you had seen the world a little. But oh, how hard it has been not to speak out all that was in my heart! And when I thought I had lost you, first to Jimmy Lufton, then to your cousin, Philippe d'Ochtè, life was very bitter, and I looked forward to years of misery and longing."

"'Way down in my heart of hearts," confessed Molly, "I knew that you cared, and the knowledge of it kept me from thinking seriously of any other man. It was awfully conceited of me to feel that way when you have never given me any real reason for it. At least, you had never written or spoken your love; but the language that is neither written nor spoken is understood by the heart, and my heart told me you loved me when my intelligence would have me understand that you did not."

"Bless your sweet heart for understanding me and speaking a good word for me! I wish my heart could have done as much for me. I could not see how you could care for me, and still I hoped and prayed. And now what is to prevent our being married right now and spending our honeymoon abroad?"

"Well, it seems to me that a young man who could possess his soul in patience for six years to find out his fate, might wait a while longer now that he knows his answer," teased Molly.

"But all my patience is gone, used up, worn out! I want you all the time to make up for this terrible nightmare of a winter that I have passed through. What is to prevent our getting married, if you really and truly care for me? Oh, Molly, be good to me! I could not stand it if the ocean separated us again!"

And Molly was good to this extent; she said: "Let's see what mother says about it."

When the pair of happy lovers reached Barbizon, they broke the news of their engagement to their friends, who had the tact to pretend to be astonished. Mrs. Brown was in a measure relieved that Molly returned the affections of the young professor. She liked him very much and fully approved of him as a son-in-law. She felt sure that he would take the best possible care of her darling daughter. There had been times when she had felt a little afraid that her advice to Edwin Green not to speak to Molly of his love until the girl had matured somewhat, was perhaps a mistake. But now, convinced that all was well, Mrs. Brown, as impulsive as ever, agreed that there was no reason to delay their marriage.

The next few days were filled with unmixed charm and delight. Barbizon was intensely interesting, having been the home of Jean François Millet. Here he lived, painted and died, the great peasant painter. The fields around the village were the scenes for the Gleaners, the Angelus, the Man with the Hoe.

The Forest, which touched the outskirts of the village, had furnished motifs for Diaz, Rousseau and Daubigny, and Judy was in a state of the greatest enthusiasm and excitement trying to spy out the exact spots where those masters of landscape had painted their pictures. Kent was delighted to follow in her footsteps and, as he expressed it, "sit at the feet of learning." He had seen but few good pictures, but he had an unerring taste in the matter of art and was able to understand Judy's ravings.

Molly and Edwin seemed to be floating above the earth. They touched ground occasionally to eat the very good food that the madame at *Maison Chevillon* served them or to pass the time of day with the other members of the party.

"Look at those two infatuated lovers, Mother," said Kent. "They look as though they had left this mundane sphere for good and all. I believe they talk in blank verse with occasional lapses into rhyme.

"'What kind er slippers do the angels wear?
   Chillun, chillun, chillun, won't yer foller me?
Don' wear none fer they tred on air,
   Hally, Hally, Hally, Hallyloodja!'"

"Nonsense, Kent, don't tease them," implored Mrs. Brown.

But strange to say, Molly did not mind the teasing she was forced to take from her brother, although Judy called him "Mr. Brown" in the most formal manner whenever he yielded to the temptation to tease her beloved Molly.

"I don't mind your calling me 'Mr. Brown' now that none of my brothers are here to answer to your endearments," laughed Kent. "I rather like it, in fact. It adds a kind of dignity to me."

They could not play around the Forest of Fontainebleau forever, much as they would have liked to. They went back to Paris a very contented, happy party: Mrs. Brown happy that her judgment had been correct in regard to her daughter's affairs; Kent and Judy happy to be in each other's society and knowing they were to have much of their chosen work ahead of them; Kent feeling almost certain that when his work was accomplished the reward awaited him, that Judy cared for him and if he could make good, would marry him; Professor Green and Molly in a seventh heaven of bliss.

Cousin Sally was immediately taken into their confidence. The news of the engagement was broken to her by Molly herself.

"Oh, what a sly-boots you were!" exclaimed the marchioness. "Philippe was right about your knowing too much about how persons ought to love not to be in love yourself. Well, my dear, I know you will be happy, and as for that Green—I hardly know how to say how happy he should be. He is not one-half so good looking as my boy, but never mind, child, I know just how clever and good and intelligent he is. He is much more suitable for you. He has the imagination that Philippe lacks. Tut—tut, I know perfectly well where my dear son falls short. There is no poetry in his make up. His father and I have often wondered at it. He looks so poetical and is all prose."

The marchioness took arrangements for the wedding into her own hands. Getting married in Paris if you happen to be foreigners, is no easy matter. There is enough red tape connected with it to reach all the way across the Atlantic; but Sally Bolling d'Ochtè was quite equal to cope with it. It took several weeks and much signing and countersigning. Birth certificates had to be obtained from Kentucky as well as baptismal certificates for Molly. The law did not seem to be so strict concerning the man.

"It does not seem fair," declared Kent. "These Frenchies will let a *man* get married without any proof of his being born; but a woman, forsooth, must first prove she is born and that she has been christened before she is allowed to enter into the holy state of matrimony."

All the papers were finally obtained, however, and Molly and her professor were married very quietly at the Protestant Episcopal Church, with no one present but the near friends and relatives. It all went as merry as a marriage bell should, but does not always go. No one wept but Polly Perkins; but Jo declared he always was a "slobber baby."

Molly naturally was married in blue, her own blue. The dressmaker almost cried when she was told that it was a wedding dress she was making, because it was not to be of white.

"Ah, the blonde bride is so wonderful and so rare! I could create for Mademoiselle a dress that would be the talk of Paris. With that hair and such fairness of complexion—well, never mind, I will still make her as beautiful as the dawn." And so she did.

After the ceremony, a wedding breakfast followed at the home of the good Cousin Sally, who felt like weeping but refrained for fear of casting a cloud on Molly's day; but it was noticed that she was especially attentive and kind to poor emotional Polly, showing that she appreciated his feelings and longed to show hers.

Molly and Edwin went on their wedding trip to—But is it kind to follow them? Let them have their solitude *à deux*. They are well able to take care of each other without our assistance.

They joined Mrs. Brown in a month and went back to Kentucky with her, leaving Judy and Kent to continue their art studies in Paris.

Judy was terribly afraid that she would have to go back under Mrs. Pace's wing when the Browns left her, but the all-capable Marchioness d'Ochtè got her a room at the American Girls' Club where she could be as free as she wished with the appearance of being well chaperoned. As for Kent he struck up quite a friendship with Pierce Kinsella, whom he had once so feared as a rival, and the two young men decided to share a studio, lessening the expense for both and heightening their pleasure.

CHAPTER XX.

MORE LETTERS.

From Mrs. Edwin Green to Miss Nance Oldham.

My dearest Nance:

Oh, Nance, I'm so happy! I wonder if any two people were ever so happy as Edwin and I. Am I not glib with my "Edwin"? I found it rather hard at first to keep from calling him Professor Green, but it seemed to mean so much to him that I have at last broken myself of the habit.

I longed for you on the day of the wedding. It did not seem right for me to take such a step without my darling Nance to help me. I was married in a traveling suit. I really believe I could not have been married in a white dress and veil unless you had been there to put on my veil.

We are having a wonderful trip, and (please don't laugh at me), but do you know it is a real privilege to travel with a man like Edwin? He knows so many things without being the least bit teachy. Mother says you are never conscious of the pedagogue in Edwin. That is really so, which I think is remarkable, considering the many persons he has to teach.

First we went to Scotland. Nothing in France thrilled me as did the lakes of Scotland. How thankful I am that, as a child, I did not have access to very many books, only the classics, and I had to read the Waverley Novels or nothing. Scotland meant a great deal more to me because of my having read Scott. Edwin says he finds about one out of ten of the young persons of the day know their Dickens and their Scott.

Edinburgh is so interesting that already Edwin and I are planning to revisit it in his next Sabbatical year. That is a long way off but we are so happy those seven years will pass quickly, I know. I almost fell over the ramparts of Edinburgh Castle trying to see the exact spot where Robert Louis Stevenson's hero, St. Ives, went down on the rope to the rocks below. As I craned my neck, Edwin whispered hoarsely in my ear: "Past yin o'cloak, and a dark, haary moarnin."

Edwin says I take fiction much more seriously than I do history. He does, too, unless the history happens to be Mary Queen of Scots or something that by rights should have been fiction. Greyfriars Bobby, for instance, is a true tale but affects us both as though it were fiction. We gave a whole afternoon to that dear little doggy, following in his footsteps as nearly as we could through the streets of Edinburgh, and out into the country by the road he took to the farm, and then back to Greyfriars Churchyard where the old shepherd, his master, was buried.

Of course we did the Burns country thoroughly. Edwin seemed as at home there as I am in the beech woods at Chatsworth. Burns has never been one of my poets, but he is now. I have adopted him for life since I realize what he means to Edwin.

We are in London now and could spend a year here and not see all we want to see. We play a splendid game which maybe you will think is silly, but you don't know how much fun it is. We pretend for a whole day to be some characters in fiction, Dickens, Thackeray, Barrie, anyone we happen to think of, and then we do the things those persons might have done. For instance, when we were slumming, I was the Marchioness and Edwin was Dick Swiveller. That was perhaps the best day of all. When we went down to the Thames embankment, Edwin suddenly turned into Rogue Riderhood and I was Lizzie Hexam.

Edwin did not think much of me as Becky Sharp when we went to the Opera nor did I think his Rawdon Crawley very convincing. His Peter Pan was splendid the afternoon we spent in Kensington Gardens, and he thought my Wendy was so perfect he tried to make me give him a "thimble" right there before all the nurse maids.

We are going home in a few days now. We are to meet Mother at Liverpool and sail from there. I do wish Mother could have done the things we have done. She would have enjoyed it so much. She laughed until she cried when I proposed her going with us. She said she loved Edwin too much and felt that he loved her too much to put his affection to such a test.

One of the very best things about being Mrs. Edwin Green is that Mother so highly approves of Edwin.

In a few weeks now we will be settled in our little Orchard Home. I hate to leave London but I long for the little home. I am a born homemaker and I am eager to get to housekeeping in the bungalow.

Edwin expects to be very busy working on a text-book on American Literature that he feels there is a need of. He does not have to go back to Wellington until January and that will give us time for lots of things in Kentucky.

When we get to Wellington, you are the first person we want to have visit us, and I want to engage you right now.

What you tell me of Andy McLean's success at Harvard does not astonish me. I was sure he would do well. I shall not be astonished either when you tell me some other news about Andy. Come on now, Nance, and 'fess up.

Good-bye.—Edwin sends his kindest regards to you and says he, too, is counting on that visit from you in January.

Yours always,

MOLLY.

Mrs. Sarah Carmichael Clay to Mrs. Mildred Carmichael Brown.

Dear Milly:

For a woman who is noted through the whole County as being the least practical person in the world, the most gullible and credulous, you certainly seem to come out at the big end of the horn.

You have managed to marry off your daughters very young, though in my opinion they are none of them beauties. Your sons seem to be able to support themselves. You have contrived to sell your birthright to an oil trust and to lift the mortgage on Chatsworth. Your servants stay with you until they die on your hands; and your friends vie with each other in rendering service to you.

I can't understand it. You must be deeper than shows on the surface. Anyhow, I take off my hat to you as being much more of a personage than I ever gave you credit for.

I am going to give Molly, for a wedding present, the portrait of our grandmother by Jouett. It is a valuable painting, so I am told, but I have had it in the attic for years as I could not bear the sight of it. You will remember it was the image of that impertinent Sally Bolling, who seemed to have the faculty of making me appear ridiculous. I never could abide her and hardly wanted to have her picture in my drawing room. I always lost sight of the fact that it was really our grandmother. I am afraid Molly is going to look like it, too.

It is high time you were coming home. Now that you have managed to marry Molly off, I should think you would have some feeling for me. My health is very poor, and certainly your duty is to look after me some and not give all of your time to your children. What with the lawsuit that I have been forced into and the constant changing of house-servants, I am in a very nervous condition.

Affectionately your sister,

SARAH CARMICHAEL CLAY.

From Professor Edwin Green to Dr. McLean at Wellington.

My dear Doctor:

I have come to the conclusion that you can take a place by the side of Dr. Weir Mitchell as one of the greatest nerve specialists of this age or any age. I am taking your prescription in large doses: deep full breaths of happiness and great brimming bowls of it. I am feeling fine and my wife says I am getting fat.

We have had a splendid trip. I have been over the same ground before, but it all seems new and wonderful to me. My wife's knowledge of your beloved Scotland put me to shame. She declares she got it all from Walter Scott and Robert Louis Stevenson and never studied a history of the country in her life.

My wife joins me in love to you and Mrs. McLean. She says that one of her chief pleasures is looking forward to having Mrs. McLean for a neighbor the rest of her life.

We will be back in Wellington after Christmas. We are now going to my wife's native state, Kentucky, where I expect to finish the textbook on American Literature that I have been pretending to work on for some time. My wife's presence will serve as inspiration to me and I hope to get ahead with it now.

Very sincerely,

EDWIN GREEN.

P. S.—My wife, using a wife's prerogative, has read this over my shoulder and declares that I may be a teacher of English, but as a writer of it I am a failure. She says she can count about a dozen "wives" in this little letter, which is very bad writing. But can you blame me? E. G.

From Caroline Jackson to Mrs. Brown.

Dear Miss Milly:

I takes my pen in hand tow enform you that most of us is enjawen pore health and hopes it finds you the same. This letter is writ for Aunt Mary Morton although the paper and awnvelop is mine, the same what Miss Molly sent me for Christmus come two yers next time. Aunt Mary wisht me tow say that she is rejicing that her Molly Baby done catch sech a fine man as her teacher pears tow be and she is praying that she will be spared tow greet them both on this side of the ribber.

We have done cleaned up Chatswuth tel you kin see yore face in mos any place you is enclined tow look. Lewis has white washed evything tel it minds me of icecreamcandyandpopcorn. Lewis has also done put in and tended the garden same as ifn you wus here. The bungleboo in the awchard is all finished and vines and flowrs growin on it same as ef it done been there fer yers.

Aunt Mary's grand darter Kizzie lows she is goin tow cook fer Miss Molly. All I kin say is Gawd hep litle Miss Molly, cause that there Kizzie is sho slow tow move and proudified (this las from me and not Aunt Mary).

Miss Sarah Clay is done had twelve cooks sence Christmus and I cyarnt count as high as the house girls run up tow. Miss Sarah is lookin right peaked and not near so buxo as formally. All of us ladies and gentlemen of African scent is rejicing that you will soon go down into the deep waters and return again once more to Kaintucky. No more at present. Plese excuse blots and a bad pen. Lewis wushes me tow add that he done furnished the stamp fer this here pistle.

Aunt Mary lows she aint long fer this here world but I knows she is still got the strenth tow make other colord folks work.

With umblest respecks,

CAROLINE JACKSON.

From Miss Julia Kean to Mrs. Edwin Green.

Molly Darling:

All day I sing: "What's this dark world to me? Molly's not here." When the wedding breakfast was over and you and your Edwin were really gone, we all of us collapsed like busted balloons. Polly

Perkins was cheerful beside the rest of us. He says he always cries at weddings. I believe he is thinking of Josephine Williams and weeps because he knows she never will marry him. I don't blame Jo, but I do feel sorry for Polly.

Your Mother and I are plunged into getting the Bents' studio in order for them. We are determined that they shall find it as shining as they left it. What a place it has been for us and how we have enjoyed it!

The d'Ochtès will soon go back to Normandy. They have asked Kent and me to visit them during the summer. Won't that be grand?

I have seen Frances Andrews several times. I never did see any one improve as she has. I think it is your influence but I know you will say it is the angle at which I am looking at her. I believe Philippe d'Ochtè is really becoming very much interested in her. I wonder what Cousin Sally will think. I fancy she will think poor Frances a far cry from her choice for her son, namely: our own Molly. I still think it is a pity we can't keep La Roche Craie in the family, but I see no way to do it.

Pierce Kinsella is painting like mad on a portrait of your mother. He says he has been crazy to paint her from the moment he laid eyes on her on the steamer. She says she rather likes posing because it means she can sit still and think. We have been in such a whirl that it might be some comfort to sit still, but I fancy I'd get enough of it in a half hour sitting.

Pierce demands only one thing of Mrs. Brown and that is that she thinks about you. He declares her expression is different.

Speaking of parents, my own are leaving Turkey to-day. Why I should keep it to the end of my letter, I don't know. I am wild with delight. It seems years since I saw them and I can hardly wait. I wish they could have got here for the wedding. Bobby always whoops things up so.

Give my best love to that most fortunate man alive; and tell him that matrimony does not mean eternal monopilization. Write to me soon at the American Girls' Club. They say it is fine and homelike there, but it will surely be some comedown after Rue Brea.

Your ever devoted,

JUDY.

Jimmy Lufton to Molly.

Press Club, New York.

My dear Mrs. Green:

Ah me! I have swallowed the bitter pill and now I am gasping for breath. I mean I have actually called you *Mrs. Green*. I did not know I was man enough to do it. One never can tell what he can do until put to the test. Anyhow, I want to congratulate both you and the Professor with all my heart. If I have to call you Mrs. Anything I believe I'd rather it would be Mrs. Green. Did you ever hear this saying?

> "Change the name and not the letter,
> Change for worse and not for better.
> Change the name and colour, too,
> Change for good and never rue."

I am sure you will "never rue" and will be as happy as you deserve, which is saying a great deal. With kindest regards to your husband (I feel myself to be a giant among men now, actually to have spoken of the Prof. as your husband!) and hoping I shall be allowed the pleasure of seeing you when you pass through New York on the way to your home in Kentucky,

I am very sincerely your friend,

JIMMY LUFTON.

From Miss Josephine Williams to Mrs. Edwin Green.

Rue Brea, Paris.

My dear Molly Brown Green:

The Bents are good friends of mine, but I must say I'll be sorry to see them back in their studio, for it will mean the departure of your wonderful mother. I truly think she has done real social settlement work in this quarter of Paris. Her influence is felt wherever she goes. For instance, I cite myself as an example. I wear trousers still, but only when I am actually at work, and I find skirts not so bad after all. As for Polly Perkins, he has actually acquired backbone enough to propose to me. I am sure your mother was at the bottom of it.

The winter bids fair to be a hard one for American artists in Paris, so I have decided that it would be wise to economize in rent. Therefore, I have consented to share a studio with Polly. Your mother is at the bottom of this move, too. Of course we have got to live, and two can live together more cheaply than they can separately. Economy of rent and fuel and light is to be considered, to say nothing of the fact that it is an impossibility to make one cup of tea or coffee. I always have a lot left in the pot and Polly might just as well have it as not. All these reasons to explain why I have said "Yes"!

Mrs. Pace bought her own portrait and has been the means of another order for poor Polly. She has also arranged to have him give some talks at her *pension* on the new movement in Art. Polly is quite spunked up and has actually had his hair cut.

The portrait of Mrs. Pace is on the whole rather interesting. I have to confess that the Cubist way of looking at her was the only way to do her justice. I think Polly was rather remarkable to see the possibilities in her.

We miss you more than I can tell you. Rue Brea seemed very lonesome at first and it took us several days to get back in our ruts.

I see a lot of your splendid young brother. I think he has been a good influence for Polly, too. He seemed to take Polly seriously and that always does a fellow good.

Pierce Kinsella is doing a wonderful portrait of your mother. It will be a sure Salon success and I bet anything will get a Mention. It has some of the qualities of Whistler's Mother. I think Pierce is one of the coming giants.

As you know by experience how difficult it is for foreigners to be married in Paris, I need not tell you of the trouble we are having to get all of my certificates from California. Polly and I can't begin our economies for several weeks yet. I should not be astonished if by that time my hair will be long enough to tuck up. Another one of your mother's touches—I'm letting it grow. Regards to the man, most blessed on earth.

Your friend,

Jo Bill.

CHAPTER XXI.

MOLLY BROWN'S ORCHARD HOME.

"Ter think er my Molly Baby back here in Kaintucky, a wedded wife with a live husband er her own! Who'd a thought it? It seems jes' a spell sence she were so teency she had to clim' on a soap box to reach up ter de dough tray ter pinch off a lil piece er yeas' dough ter make her play rolls wif, so she an' that there Kent could have a party in de ole apple tree they called ther carstle. An' now de carstle done blowed down an' in a twinklin' of de eye, most fo' dis ole nigger could tun 'round, here is a sho nuf house whar de carstle stood an' my lil baby chile is mistress here wif a dough tray an' bis'it board er her own, an' now," and here Aunt Mary paused to give one of her inimitable chuckles, "she don' have ter stretch up none ter reach de table but has to ben' over right smart in de tother d'rection."

"Don't you think our bungalow is lovely?" asked Molly, who looked very pretty in her cap and apron as she bent over her own biscuit board cutting out tiny biscuit, the kind that Edwin liked best, ready to bake for breakfast.

"Yes, chile, it is a fittin' home for the likes of you; but fer the land's sake, don' call it no sich a name as that there! It makes me think er hants. It soun's too like bugger-boo ter me. Jes' call it house or home, but not dat scary name what you and yo' teacher roll out so keerless like."

"All right, Aunt Mary, if you don't like bungalow, 'my teacher' and I will stop calling it that."

Molly popped the biscuit into the oven, put the sliced bacon on the griddle, tested her coffee to see if it had percolated sufficiently, got the butter and cream out of the refrigerator, cracked ice to put in the cantaloupe, and made a pitcher of ice water before it was time to turn the bacon.

"Sakes alive, chile, how you kin tun aroun'! That there Ca'line would a bin a hour doin' what you done 'complished in a few minutes."

Just then Professor Green came into the kitchen, hunting Molly, whom he could not let out of his sight for very long.

"Well, Aunt Mary, I am so glad to see you," and he shook hands with the old woman. "My wife tells me that you are to spend the day with us, also that your granddaughter, Kizzie, is coming to cook for us. Just look at my wife, Aunt Mary, isn't she the most beautiful wife in all the world?"

He proceeded to embrace Molly, dish towel, coffee pot and all. Molly put the coffee pot down by the ice water, dropped the dish towel into the wood box and allowed herself to be kissed, laughing gayly at the old darkey's expression of amusement.

"Oh, yes, wife, wife, wife! That's all one er these here green husbands kin say. But I see right here ef I *is* comp'ny done come to spen' de day, I'd bes' put on a ap'on and git ter wuck. De bac'n is ready ter burn up and I 'low that there pan er baby bis'it is done to a turn. De coffee pot done het up de ice water and de ice water done took the 'roma from de coffee. Here I was a passin' compliments on Miss Molly 'bout her swif'ness, and she actin' jes lak Ca'line! De kitchen ain't no place fer spoons, 'less they is i'on spoons to stir up de batter wif. Go 'long an' sit down in yo' cheers. I'll bring in the victuals."

Aunt Mary was very strict with the other servants and would have reprimanded any of them severely for venturing a remark "while de white folks was eatin'," but she followed Molly and Edwin to the screened porch where the table was laid, and while they ate the very good breakfast which, thanks to her, had not burned up, the old woman entertained them with her keen observations.

"I knowed you'd be pleased wif de Jonases gourd I done planted hin' de kitchen on that arbor what Mr. Kent called by some outlandish name lak perg'low. I say I planted de gourd, which ain't ter say the wholesome truf. Yer see, gourds mus' be planted by a foolish 'ooman or a lazy, no-'count man ef you want 'em to grow fas'. I sho did want that there vine to kiver de arbor befo' you and yo' teacher got here, so I got Ca'line, who is 'thout doubt the foolishest virgin I ever seed, to plant on one side and that low down, lazy Buck Jasper to tend to tother, and you kin see fer yo'self they's meetin' overhead."

"The vine has certainly grown very rapidly," laughed the professor. "I have never heard before what were the requisites for a flourishing gourd."

"Well, I ain't a-sayin' that part of its comin' on so well ain't due to the haid work that old Mary Morton put on it. I bossed them free niggers till they done disremembered they was 'mancipated."

"What would you say, Aunt Mary, if Kent should bring a wife back to Chatsworth?" asked Molly.

"Well, if it is that there Judy gal, I'd say, 'Glory be!' She's sho jes' lak our own folks, if she do say her ma and pa ain't never owned they own home, but always been renters. That don' sound zactly lak quality, but since the war, that ain't sich a sho sign as it uster be. You see plenty er po' white trash now a-ownin' fine homes and de quality rentin' nothin' mo' than cabins."

"Well, Judy is the gal I mean, Aunt Mary, and I fancy they will come to live with Mother at Chatsworth."

"Don' it beat all how Miss Milly's daughters is marryin' out and her sons a-marryin' in? I done heard Miss Milly say hunderds er times that she'd 'low her daughters to marry in but her sons must marry out, as daughters-in-law is heaps mo' ticklish to git 'long wif than sons-in-law. Here her three daughters is a marryin' an' going to all kin's er outlan'ish places leavin' they ma an' they home; an' now the boys is thinkin' bout takin' unto theyselves wives, an' one an' all say they can't sleep nowheres but at Chatsworth, an' they mus' bring they wives back home to keep comp'ny wif yo' ma! Mr. Paul's cou'tin' 'round, but he manages to git stuck on too many gals at oncet and makes it hard to settle hisself. I done noticed, howsomever, 'bout that kinder whimsified lover, when he do settle down, he makes the bes' husband er all. Men folks is gotter have they fling, and they bes' have it 'fo' matrimony than durin' it.

"Dr. John was right hard hit wif that Miss Hunt what was a-visiting yo' Aunt Clay 'til he seed her wif her hair all stringy an' out er curl that time you all went on the night picnic and the creek riz so and mos' drownded the passel of you. He ain't never paid no 'tention to her since; but they do tell me that pretty, rosy-cheeked young lady he drove out here las' week from Lou'ville is liable to be Mrs. Dr. John. What's mo', Ca'line tells me she is a trained nurse. She certainly do look lak a lady and I tuck notice she eat lak a lady, ef she does hire herself out in service. Pears lak to me that the mo' things the niggers thinks theyselves too good to do, the mo' things the white folks decide they ain't too good ter do fer theyselves."

"Why, Aunt Mary, of course Miss Graves is a lady. She belongs to one of the very best families and is very well educated and certainly charming and sweet. John will be lucky, indeed, if he can persuade her to have him."

"Well, honey chile, ef you say so, 'tis so. 'Cose in days gone by a nuss was a nuss, cep' some was good and some was bad, but now it seems some is ladies an' some ain't."

"Here comes Mother," exclaimed Edwin, springing from his seat to go meet his mother-in-law, who was opening the neat little green gate that connected the Chatsworth gardens with the old orchard where he had built his nest.

"What lazy children, just having breakfast! I feel as though I had eaten mine ages ago, and yours looks so good, I believe I'll have some more,—just a cup of coffee and a biscuit. Aunt Mary, you have made a better cook of your Molly Baby than you have of Caroline. I never have such biscuit as these except when you come to spend the day."

Aunt Mary had become so feeble that she was not able to do steady work. She lived in a comfortable cabin at the foot of the hill, making frequent excursions to the "great house" to see that "the niggers was 'memberin' they places and that that there Ca'line wan't sleepin' out er season."

"Well, Miss Milly, it's jes' this way: some folks is good slow cooks an' some is good quick cooks. Now Ca'line shines when slow patience is the needcessity. She is great on a biled dinner, where the 'gredients have to jes' simper along. You have her make a Brunswick stew an' you'll think she is the bes' cook in the county. Her yeas' bread is good 'cause that takes time and Ca'line is twins to whatsoever takes time; but ef you have a steak to brile or quick bis'it to cook, you jes sen' fer this ole woman, an' ef she can't crawl up the hill she kin ketch holt er President's tail an' he kin pull her up."

Aunt Mary then busied herself clearing off the table, as her way of spending the day was to help her hostess in many ways.

What a peaceful picture the orchard home presents on this late summer morning! The little brown bungalow looks as though it had always been there. The trees are laden with apples. The fall cheeses are beginning to ripen, and the wine saps are so heavy that Edwin has proudly propped up the bending boughs. The quickly growing vines have done their best for the newly-wedded pair, and the slower ivy has begun to send out shoots that need daily training with matting tacks until they accustom themselves to sticking to the stone foundations. Molly's porch boxes are filled with nasturtiums and petunias, and on each side of the steps are beds of scarlet sage.

Her sister Sue drove over to the orchard as soon as the news came of Molly's approaching wedding, and superintended the planting of many flowers to beautify the little home; and even stern old Aunt Clay unbent to the extent of lending her gardener to do the work. She had also donated a clump of Adam's and Eve's needles and threads that proved very decorative, but quite as unapproachable as Aunt Clay herself.

"It is a splendid apple year," remarked Mrs. Brown, her eyes wandering over the bountifully laden trees. "Do you know, Edwin, I believe you will realize enough off your wine saps and pippins to pay for all your furniture!"

"It is all paid for, thank goodness!" laughed the young man. "But the apple money is to be put in the bank in Molly's account."

"You remember when I went to college, Mother, you said I must win the three golden apples. Don't you think apple money in the bank is a golden apple?"

"Yes, my child, perhaps it is; but happiness is a bigger and more golden apple than money in the bank, and I believe you have gained happiness."

"Indeed I have," said Molly blushing. "And now I am going to make a pie for my own husband; out of my own apples; off my own tree; in my own kitchen; with my own hands; and before I go, I am going to hug the old man who bought the orchard so I could go on with my college education."

This time Edwin did not "bow his head and wait 'til the storm passed over him" as he had, according to Molly, in years gone by; but he drew her down on the arm of his chair, and the making of the famous pie had to be postponed.

The pie was finally made, though, and an extra one to send over to Mother. Aunt Mary declared it was the "bestest I ever set gum in. I uster have a sweet tooth, but now I ain't got nothin' but a sweet gum; but my Molly Baby kin make sich good crus' th' ain't no need to chaw none."

The old woman had been rather scornful of the method of making pastry that Molly had learned from the domestic science teacher at Wellington, but when the pie turned out such a success she was converted.

"Yo' teacher is sho' done drawd a prize cook. The two things what men folks think the mos' of is the gal's outsides an' they own insides. The gal's outsides is goin' to change an' fade; but ef she's got sense 'nuf ter keep on a caterin' ter his insides, the man ain't a gwine ter notice the change. Ain't that the truf?" she asked Edwin as he came into the kitchen hunting his Molly.

"You know best, Aunt Mary. Certainly this pie would hide a multitude of wrinkles and even gray hair. But now, Aunt Mary, can't you persuade my wife to leave the kitchen long enough to come take a little walk with me?"

"Go long with him, chile. I reckon I can keep the bungleboo from flyin' off while you an' yo' teacher takes a little ex'cise."

So Molly took off her cap and apron and, donning a shade hat, stepped joyfully out in the sunshine with her husband. They followed the little brook at the foot of the orchard, and climbing the fence, found themselves once more in the beechwoods. Both of them remembered the walk they had taken there together more than two years before, and with one accord they directed their footsteps to the great tree, the father of the forest, where they had sat on that memorable walk.

> "'Of all the beautiful pictures
> That hang on Memory's wall,
> Is one of a dim, old forest
> That seemeth the best of all.'

"Do you remember, Dearest, how you quoted that poem to me when we walked here before?" asked Edwin, drawing Molly to him.

"Yes, I remember quite well," said Molly. "I also remember what you said, but I am afraid it will make you conceited if I tell you. It is a long time to remember something that is not poetry."

"Please tell me. If I ever said anything that was worth remembering that long, you should encourage me by telling it to me."

"You said: 'A beautiful picture comes to my inward eye, and that is an old Molly with white hair sitting where you are now, still in the romantic era, still in the beechwoods; and God willing, I'll be beside you.' I have thought of those words very often, and when I wasn't certain that you really cared for me, I would say to myself that you must have cared then." And Molly blushed.

"Cared for you! I can't see how I ever kept from telling you that day. It is best as it is. You were too young, but sometimes even now when I know you are mine, I tremble to think that I might have lost you by waiting."

"There was never any real danger of that. If you had not cared, I was determined to be an old maid." And Molly gave a sigh of happiness as she nestled close to her "teacher."

The quiet and peace of the "Orchard Home" seemed too perfect to be disturbed even by the uneasy mutterings of distant war clouds. But as time passed and the chill forebodings and grim shadows of war reached the most secluded and sacred spots in the world, so they came, too, as we shall see, into the home and into the life of "Molly Brown of Kentucky."

THE END

THE Ann Sterling Series

By HARRIET PYNE GROVE

Stories of Ranch and College Life
For Girls 12 to 16 Years

ANN STERLING

The strange gift of Old Never-Run, an Indian whom she has befriended, brings exciting events into Ann's life.

THE COURAGE OF ANN

Ann makes many new, worthwhile friends during her first year at Forest Hill College.

ANN AND THE JOLLY SIX

At the close of their Freshman year Ann and the Jolly Six enjoy a house party at the Sterling's mountain ranch.

ANN CROSSES A SECRET TRAIL

The Sterling family, with a group of friends, spend a thrilling vacation under the southern Pines of Florida.

ANN'S SEARCH REWARDED

In solving the disappearance of her father, Ann finds exciting adventures, Indians and bandits in the West.

ANN'S AMBITIONS

The end of her Senior year at Forest Hill brings a whirl of new events into the career of "Ann of the Singing Fingers."

ANN'S STERLING HEART

Ann returns home, after completing a busy year of musical study abroad.

Books for Girls

By GRACE MAY NORTH

Author of THE VIRGINIA DAVIS SERIES

MEG OF MYSTERY MOUNTAIN

This story tells of the summer vacation some young people spent in the mountains and how they cleared up the mystery of the lost cabin at Crazy Creek Mine.

RILLA OF THE LIGHTHOUSE

"Rilla" had lived all her life with only her grandfather and "Uncle Barney" as companions, but finally, at High Cliff Seminary, her great test came and the lovable girl from Windy Island Lighthouse met it brilliantly.

NAN OF THE GYPSIES

In this tale of a wandering gypsy band, Nan, who has spent her childhood with the gypsies, is adopted by a woman of wealth, and by her love and loyalty to her, she proves her fine character and true worth.

SISTERS

The personal characteristics and incidents in the lives of two girls — one thoughtless and proud, the other devoted and self-sacrificing — are vividly described in this story, told as it is with sympathy and understanding for both.

The Camp Fire Girls Series

By HILDEGARD G. FREY

A Series of Outdoor Stories for
Girls 12 to 16 Years.

THE CAMP FIRE GIRLS IN THE MAINE WOODS;
or, The Winnebagos go Camping.

THE CAMP FIRE GIRLS AT SCHOOL; or, The
Wohelo Weavers.

THE CAMP FIRE GIRLS AT ONOWAY HOUSE; or,
The Magic Garden.

THE CAMP FIRE GIRLS GO MOTORING; or, Along
the Road That Leads the Way.

THE CAMP FIRE GIRLS' LARKS AND PRANKS; or,
The House of the Open Door.

THE CAMP FIRE GIRLS ON ELLEN'S ISLE; or, The
Trail of the Seven Cedars.

THE CAMP FIRE GIRLS ON THE OPEN ROAD;
or, Glorify Work.

THE CAMP FIRE GIRLS DO THEIR BIT; or, Over
the Top with the Winnebagos.

THE CAMP FIRE GIRLS SOLVE A MYSTERY; or,
The Christmas Adventure at Carver House.

THE CAMP FIRE GIRLS AT CAMP KEEWAYDIN;
or, Down Paddles.

The Girl Scouts Series

BY EDITH LAVELL

A new copyright series of Girl Scouts stories by an author of wide
experience in Scouts' craft, as Director of Girl Scouts of Philadelphia.

THE GIRL SCOUTS AT MISS ALLENS SCHOOL

THE GIRL SCOUTS AT CAMP

THE GIRL SCOUTS' GOOD TURN

THE GIRL SCOUTS' CANOE TRIP

THE GIRL SCOUTS' RIVALS

THE GIRL SCOUTS ON THE RANCH

THE GIRL SCOUTS' VACATION ADVENTURES

THE GIRL SCOUTS' MOTOR TRIP

THE GIRL SCOUTS' CAPTAIN

THE GIRL SCOUTS' DIRECTOR

The Greycliff Girls Series

By HARRIET PYNE GROVE

Stories of Adventure, Fun, Study and Personalities of girls attending
Greycliff School.
For Girls 10 to 15 Years

CATHALINA AT GREYCLIFF

THE GIRLS OF GREYCLIFF

GREYCLIFF WINGS

GREYCLIFF GIRLS IN CAMP

GREYCLIFF HEROINES

GREYCLIFF GIRLS IN GEORGIA

GREYCLIFF GIRLS' RANCHING

GREYCLIFF GIRLS' GREAT ADVENTURE

Molly Brown's Orchard Home

Marjorie Dean High School Series

BY PAULINE LESTER

Author of the Famous Marjorie Dean College Series

These are clean, wholesome stories that will be of great interest to all girls of high school age.

MARJORIE DEAN, HIGH SCHOOL FRESHMAN

MARJORIE DEAN, HIGH SCHOOL SOPHOMORE

MARJORIE DEAN, HIGH SCHOOL JUNIOR

MARJORIE DEAN, HIGH SCHOOL SENIOR

THE MERRY LYNN SERIES

By HARRIET PYNE GROVE

The charm of school and camp life, outdoor sports and European travel is found in these winning tales of Merilyn and her friends at boarding school and college. These realistic stories of the everyday life, the fun, frolic and special adventures of the Beechwood girls will be enjoyed by all girls of high school age.

MERILYN ENTERS BEECHWOLD

MERILYN AT CAMP MEENAHGA

MERILYN TESTS LOYALTY

MERILYN'S NEW ADVENTURE

MERILYN FORRESTER, CO-ED.

THE "MERRY LYNN" MINE

The Virginia Davis Series

By GRACE MAY NORTH

Clean, Wholesome Stories of Ranch Life.
For Girls 12 to 16 Years.

VIRGINIA OF V. M. RANCH

VIRGINIA AT VINE HAVEN

VIRGINIA'S ADVENTURE CLUB

VIRGINIA'S RANCH NEIGHBORS

VIRGINIA'S ROMANCE

Princess Polly Series

By AMY BROOKS

Author of "Dorothy Dainty" series, Etc.

Stories of Sweet-Tempered, Sunny, Lovable Little "Princess Polly."
For girls 12 to 16 years.

PRINCESS POLLY

PRINCESS POLLY'S PLAYMATES

PRINCESS POLLY AT SCHOOL

PRINCESS POLLY BY THE SEA

PRINCESS POLLY'S GAY WINTER

PRINCESS POLLY AT PLAY

PRINCESS POLLY AT CLIFFMORE

9 781034 823681